M$. Fortune

Kandy Witte

This book is a work of fiction. Names, characters, places and incidents are either products of the author's imagination or used fictitiously. Any resemblance to actual events, locales, or persons, living or dead, is entirely coincidental. All rights reserved. No part of this publication can be reproduced or transmitted in any form or by any means, electronic or mechanical, without permission in writing from the author or publisher.

ACKNOWLEDGEMENTS

I wish to thank my family, my friends of the Cozy Book Club and my fellow writers of the Ohio Valley Writers Network. Special thanks also to everyone who offered the feedback and insights that helped make Merry June the woman she is today.

I can be reached at wittsendpress@gmail.com and look forward to hearing from readers. I will forward all compliments to Merry June and all criticisms to Harold.

Kandy

For My Grandson, With Love

ONE

Merry June checked her watch. One minute later than the last time she looked. Harold pretended not to notice. He sipped his coffee and flipped to the sports section.

"Harold, are you done here?"

Harold drained his cup and with one finger, pushed it across the dining room table. He lowered the paper and glared at his wife. "Happy?"

"Oh, yeah, Harold. Livin' the dream, livin' the dream."

She whisked the cup, the creamer and the plate of chocolate chip cookie crumbs off to the kitchen where she flipped on the portable television set. It was a nightly ritual with the Piggs; Harold waited until the last minute to finish his after-dinner coffee and Merry June raced to the kitchen just in time to catch the opening sequence of her very favorite show, *Fortune Hunt*.

For thirty-minutes, five nights a week, Merry June

was transported from the farm in Shandon, Ohio, to the glitter and thrill of Hollywood. Sitting in her kitchen, with the faded yellow paint and her collection of milk glass, she was not just a wife and grandmother but a contestant on the set of the most popular game show on television.

She loved everything about the program. Each night she competed with the four contestants as they faced off in a *fortune hunt* by vying to answer questions in a wide range of categories.

As much as she loved challenging herself with the questions, Merry June loved the fact that the show's host was a woman. Willow, looking like a movie star in gowns and accessories worthy of an appearance on the red carpet, was intelligent and funny and if Merry June ever wished she could trade places with someone—and to be honest, sometimes she did—it would be Willow, hands down.

She picked up the black cat that had wandered into the room and was rubbing against her leg. "Come on, Maizy, it's time for our show." She turned up the sound and leaned in close to the screen. The first contestant selected a square to reveal the category, 'The Bible'. Merry June whispered in the cat's ear, "Bring it on. We've got this!"

"For one hundred dollars," Willow said tapping the square again to uncover the question, "who was Israel's firstborn son?"

"Too easy," Merry June snorted. "Reuben, of course."

"Reuben is correct," Willow said. She smiled at the male contestant and instructed him to pick another category.

"Come on 'bag of gold'!" Merry June urged the contestant to find the single square that revealed the sack with gold coins spilling out. The right answer to the mystery category hidden there could win the lucky player $100,000.

"Oh rats, not 'Opera'! I never get 'Opera'," Merry June yelled when the category behind another colored square appeared.

"Who composed the opera *Nixon in China*?" she read off the screen. "For a measly fifty dollars? That's an opera? You've got to be kidding." Merry June choked when the player guessed the answer as John Adams. "Oh, sure, buddy," she snickered, "why not George Washington?"

"John Adams is correct," Willow said.

Merry June groaned and when an ad came on featuring a couple in bathtubs on a deserted beach, she

3

turned the sound to 'mute'. She massaged her aching knees and stood up to stretch.

"Come on, Maizy. We better check on your dad." She nuzzled the top of the animal's head. "Maybe we could interest him in a bath." She smiled as she pictured Harold squeezing his bulky six-foot frame into their narrow tub. "Or maybe not."

She peeked into the living room where her husband of fifty years lay sprawled in the recliner for his customary post-prandial nap while pretending to watch PBS NewsHour. The cat jumped out of Merry June's arms onto Harold's wide lap, curled into a ball and fell asleep. Assured that everything was business as usual in the Pigg household, Merry June retrieved the bottle of Mogen David wine she kept stashed in the cabinet with her Christmas mugs, and poured a drink.

She took a sip and let her mind wander to the list of tasks for the week ahead; tonight, she'd finish folding the laundry, put aside the pieces that needed ironing for tomorrow and set out the pork chops to thaw for Tuesday's dinner. *Maybe I'll shake things up and switch Tuesday's pork chops for Wednesday's meatloaf or Friday's tuna casserole. Harold would be apoplectic and that might be fun.* She pictured the scene; Harold stomping off to the barn or the garden or burying his head in a National Geographic magazine until she, overcome with guilt, would bring him a sandwich with milk and cookies as a peace offering. *On second thought, I'm not up for the drama, not this week.*

She poured a second glass of wine and gazed upward at a framed needlepoint that hung over the sink, a quotation by Mark Twain that had been a graduation gift from her grandmother. Merry June had adored the woman who outlived three husbands, joined the Peace Corps at seventy and died of a heart attack on a cruise with her ninety-year-old boyfriend.

She ran her eyes over the words she had inscribed on her heart so long ago, made more meaningful with time:

"Twenty years from now you will be more disappointed by the things that you didn't do than by the ones you did do. So, throw off the bowlines. Sail away from the safe harbor. Catch the trade winds in your sails. Explore. Dream. Discover."

"It took me longer than I planned, Grandma," she said to the vision in her mind, "but Merry June Pigg is about to set sail."

TWO

Merry June squeezed her eyes shut and pictured herself in the dress she'd purchased for the upcoming party. It was like a peach chiffon she'd seen Willow wear but the skirt on Merry June's was tea-length and instead of sequins, the bodice was fabric with soft folds flowing from the neckline. She felt like a teenager getting ready for prom—or maybe an older version of Willow herself. But what made her smile and gave her shivers, were the shoes; clear plastic pumps with two-inch heels, a thin, ankle strap studded with tiny rhinestones and a matching bow that set off the toes and glittered when she held them to the light.

The shindig, as Harold referred to the event, was a gift from their children, Rob and Allison, to celebrate her seventieth birthday and the couple's Golden Wedding Anniversary that fell on the same day. Merry June would have preferred a small family gathering at home rather than the fancy party at the Cincinnati Club but both she and Harold would have set each other's hair on fire rather than disappoint their children. Instead, they pasted on smiles and pretended to be pleased—except when they were alone.

The anniversary couple had barely spoken all week. Their argument started when Merry June showed Harold her new dress and shoes. "You can't be serious," he scoffed. "You're not some teenager—you're a seventy-year-old woman, a Sunday school teacher, for God's sake. And those shoes? Just don't come running to me if you fall and break a hip."

"I wanted to look nice for our party, Harold." She fought back tears and tried to keep her voice level. "We need to get you a suit…"

"No, we don't," he exploded. "Why do you want to truss me up like a damned Christmas goose? I'll be in my workshop." He opened the door to the basement. "I think I'll just take off all my damn clothes. I think I'll become a damn nudist," he shouted before slamming the door behind him.

Merry June snapped. She jerked the door open and yelled down the stairs, "I may be a seventy-year-old grandma but that doesn't mean I have to wear polyester pantsuits and orthopedic shoes." She slammed the door then yanked it back open and shouted an afterthought, "And if you die first, I'm gonna bury you in a tuxedo so you have to spend eternity in a cummerbund and bow tie. Put that in your pipe, mister!"

She slammed the door again and marched to the kitchen where she consoled herself with a large slice of the cake she'd baked for her only grandchild, sixteen-year-old Noah. She was so upset she licked the gooey chocolate frosting from her fingers instead of washing up properly. *I wish this party were over*. She wiped away a tear.

It wasn't that she didn't believe in celebrating life's special milestones, it was just so darn exhausting and stressful. Then there would be an argument over the suit and her mind was on more important things than dressing up Harold. When he retired from his job as head of security for the V.A. hospital in Cincinnati, her husband took every suit and tie he had to Goodwill and replaced them with tee shirts and jeans. He swore the only thing that would ever go around his neck again would be the noose they'd hang him with when he killed the next person who tried to get him to put on a tie.

M$. FORTUNE

Harold reveled in retirement. He loved nothing more than working on projects around the house and on an old farm there was always something that needed attention. He was even studying up on canning and preserving the fruits and vegetables he nursed from seeds in early spring until the last zucchini was harvested in the fall. In bad weather when he couldn't work outside, he'd spend his days in his basement woodworking shop where he turned out handcrafted toys and jewelry boxes. After he threw away the stainless- steel Timex that had been a retirement gift from the hospital administrator, he'd crafted a beautiful grandfather clock that he placed in their foyer. He told Merry June that if he ever needed to know the time of day, which would only happen if a Reds game was being televised, the clock was far superior to a steel band around his wrist that reminded him of a handcuff to his former, regimented life.

Her husband found satisfaction in the new life he'd made for himself, but Merry June had grown restless. Of course, she enjoyed her family and friends, her book club, the volunteer work at church and an occasional substitute-teaching job at the school where she'd taught for twenty-five years. Most of the time, she thought of herself as a happy person and was content with the life she'd chosen. Even last year, when she discovered a lump in her breast, she was the one who kept everybody else's spirits up. Fortunately, it turned out to be a cyst and was removed without fanfare, but the scare forced her to examine her life in a new light and made her face her own mortality in a way she hadn't before. This birthday was the alarm on her biological clock and she was finally waking up.

THREE

When the family arrived at the Cincinnati Club, Harold wasn't speaking to Merry June and Harold had been such a sourpuss nobody was speaking to him. Rob dropped them off at the door and once inside, Merry June told Harold she had to stop at the restroom and would catch up with him.

She waited until the elevator door closed before she went to the baggage checkroom. "I left two bags here yesterday," she told the young woman behind the desk. "I'll be down to pick them up at eleven o'clock sharp, so will you make sure they'll be waiting for me?"

The woman checked the claim stubs. "Got it. I'll make sure you're good to go."

...

Merry June soaped her hands and arms all the way to her

elbows and sang the song she'd made up for Noah, when he was a toddler; *I wash my hands all day long, I wash my hands and I sing this song, I'm clean, germ free, I'm clean—that's me!* She threw her hands into the air for the grand finish and repeated the washing and the song two more times.

A woman she recognized from the Agape Circle at church stopped to apply fresh lipstick. "Enjoying your party?"

Merry June pulled down paper towels for each hand before she answered, "This will be a night I'll never forget."

She took her time drying each finger, then the palms and finally the back of each hand. She wrapped a paper towel around her hand and pulled the door open. She smiled down at the sparkling bows on her pumps and glided into Ballroom C where an Elvis impersonator sang, *My Way*.

...

"And now, let's give a big round of applause to these two lovebirds, Mr. and Mrs. Pigg." Elvis held out his hand to Merry June.

Harold stood stiff and red faced beside his wife. He gripped a martini in one hand and a card in the other.

12

He nodded at Merry June and emptied his drink with one swallow. He held up his empty glass and motioned for the waiter to bring him another.

Merry June knew her husband would rather be at home running his callused fingers along the soft and hard woods in his shop. *Harold is like his woodworking, she thought, solid and reliable if not always fashionable.* Her heart went out to him as she watched him work on a smile that looked more like a grimace and felt her stomach do a somersault.

Harold downed his fresh martini bringing catcalls and laughter from the audience. Rob took the empty glass, glared at his father and gave him a hard push toward Merry June. He whispered something in Harold's ear before he exited the stage.

Merry June reached out to take her husband's hand and gave him a smile of encouragement. He looked like a man who had dressed up for his own execution. He'd opened the top buttons of his new polo shirt and loosened his belt. His face was red from the martinis and the card he held was twisted and damp in his sweaty hands.

"Merry June," he began, staring at his feet, "Happy Anniversary, I mean, uh, Happy Birthday." He thrust the

13

card at her and leaned forward to kiss her cheek.

She put the card into her evening bag. She looked at the upturned faces of her children—Allison wiped away a tear and Rob forced a smile. Noah mouthed the words, 'love you, Grandma,' and gave her the thumb's up that was their special sign.

"Thank you all for coming to help us celebrate this very special occasion," she said, her voice strong. "Fifty years is a long time." Encouraged by laughter from the crowd, she became even more confident. "I was just a baby when I married Harold. We met my senior year of college on a blind date and eloped on my birthday three months later."

Her friends cheered her on.

"I married Harold for love—and money," she said and grinned. "Then, as the saying goes, I found out he lied about the money." Hoots and claps prodded her to continue. Harold's face got redder. He took off his belt and stuffed it in his pocket.

"That was okay, because soon we were blessed with Rob, then Allison and now our family includes our beautiful daughter-in-law, Jane, and of course, our brilliant grandson, Noah, who," she paused to blow Noah a kiss, "will become rich enough to throw me another

14

great party for my one-hundredth birthday."

"Right on, Grandma." Noah jumped up and planted a big kiss on her cheek. "Have a great trip. Don't forget, you promised to text me at least once every single day," he whispered in her ear before he rejoined his parents.

Somebody pushed Harold and Merry June together for a dance as Elvis crooned *Memories*. Merry June felt Harold squeeze her hand and tighten his arm around her waist. They finished the dance holding each other close. *The old boy still knows how to get to me. Why did he have to get romantic now?* She pulled away from her husband and gave a little curtsey.

"Guess I'll go look for Conny," she said, referring to her neighbor and best friend. "And cake."

"Okay. See you later." He looked embarrassed and dug his fists into the pockets of his new pants.

Merry June touched his hands. "Don't do that. You'll stretch..."

He turned on his heel and headed for the bar.

...

The cake was a three-layered chocolate affair with frothy white icing and Disney characters that danced around each tier. On top, Mickey Mouse wore a party hat and blew into a noisemaker. "Make mine a big piece," she

15

instructed the server. "And some champagne too, please?"

Conny came up beside her. "Having fun?"

Merry June, her mouth full, could only nod and smile in reply. Conny helped herself to cake and led her friend towards a corner table away from the noise and people.

They sat for a while enjoying the quiet until Conny finally spoke, "Are you okay?"

Merry June put down her fork and took both of her best friend's hands in her own. "You are the sister I never had. I love you with all my heart."

"Me too."

"I am in a conundrum," Merry June said.

Conny waited.

"In all the years I've known you, I have never lied to you or kept anything from you."

"I know. Me either."

"What if I say for the first time ever, I've kept the biggest thing I've ever done from you?"

Conny started to laugh but sensing her friend was serious, she hesitated before she answered, "What if the tables were turned? What if I had this big secret, would you want me to tell you?"

"Of course!"

"There's your answer."

A server brought two glasses of champagne. Merry June held up her glass and Conny did the same. "Here's to our friendship," Merry June said, "and to my safe journey." She clicked her glass against her friend's and added, "Because tonight, I'm running away from home."

FOUR

"Merry June Pigg, are you telling me you're leaving Harold?"

"Yes, I mean, no." She felt sillier by the minute.

Conny motioned to a server and asked her to bring them a whole bottle of champagne.

Fortified by the alcohol, Merry June went on to explain. "I am leaving," she said, "but not for good. A week, maybe a bit longer, but probably less. It depends."

Conny threw back her head and finished her drink in one swallow. She set her glass on the table and motioned to Merry June for a refill. "You are not making any sense. What in the world are you talking about?"

Merry June stared down at her new shoes, admiring how the lights made the rhinestone bows sparkle. She straightened her necklace, sat up in her chair and announced, "I'm giving myself a present for my birthday.

I'm going to Los Angeles to audition for..."

"*Fortune*...?"

"Yes," Merry June jumped in excitedly. "You know how I play along every night and you and Ed and even Harold said I was as good if not better than most of the people who go on." She sat back, flushed, and waited for her announcement to sink in as Conny digested the news. "I didn't want to say anything until the last minute because I was afraid I wouldn't go through with it and there I'd be with egg all over my face." She waited for her friend to say something and when she didn't, Merry June continued, "I've been thinking about this since last year."

"This is all very funny. You're going to California— you who have never been any further than Indianapolis? To try out for the most popular show on television? And you are actually expecting me to believe that Harold...?"

"I'm leaving tonight," Merry June interrupted. "I guess you think I've lost my marbles. I know it sounds silly."

"Silly doesn't begin to describe it. Silly is the time you dyed your hair red thinking you'd look like Lucille Ball. Silly is when you sewed Harold a powder blue, polyester leisure suit, without a fly, and then, to top it off, you made Rob a matching one. Now those were silly," Conny said laughing. "But this is just downright crazy."

"You've had your moments, too. What about the time you tried to re-create a Martha Stewart Thanksgiving and ended up setting fire to your dining room with your handcrafted chandelier and homemade candles?" Merry June said. She wiped away the tears rolling down her cheeks.

"True. But those were nothing compared to what you're talking about." Conny sat back and studied her friend closely. "You're pulling my leg, aren't you? You almost had me there, I admit it."

"I'm not kidding. I've been thinking about this for a while. This isn't just a whim." She took her friend's hand. "Remember last year when I found that lump?"

"Of course. That was terrifying."

"I've never been so scared. It made me reflect on my life and how fortunate I've been. I have family and friends I love," she said, and squeezed her friend's hand. "And people who love me. I've been truly blessed, but..."

"But?"

"I realized I've never gone beyond my safe, comfortable life in Shandon, Ohio. I started to wonder if this is all I'm ever going to be? Dull, responsible Merry June Pigg. And you know what?"

Conny shook her head.

"I decided that's not how I want Noah to remember me. I want him to remember me as somebody who dared to take a chance, to follow a dream as crazy as it may be. I want to inspire him the way my grandma inspired me. And, not only that," she paused and took a deep breath, "I want an adventure."

Conny rubbed her temples before she answered, "Okay, let's say for the sake of argument I get all that. How do you know they'll even let you audition? There must be thousands of people who want to try out."

"I sent in a video application…"

"A video? What have you done with Merry June? The woman who still has a camera that uses film?"

"I had a little help from Noah," she admitted.

"I can't believe Harold is willing to go along with this."

Merry June paused and studied her clasped hands. "Harold hasn't exactly gone along with it."

"What do you mean?

"I haven't exactly told him yet."

Conny got so excited she pushed her unfinished plate of cake away. "You haven't EXACTLY told him? What EXACTLY have you told him?"

"I told him if he wanted to get me a birthday gift, I'd

21

rather have cash."

Conny dropped her head into her hands. She squinted at Merry June from between her fingers. "Let me get this straight. You're running out on your family and friends at your own party. Even though your chances are slim to none, you hope to land a spot on *Fortune Hunt*. You'll be gone for a week—maybe longer. And, your husband of fifty years doesn't know?"

"That pretty well sums it up," Merry June said. Her eyes watered and she twisted the chiffon skirt of her dress. "But, I did tell Noah. He made me promise to call him every day or he was going to spill the beans."

"Then Allison and Rob don't know either?"

Mary June frowned, "Rob would probably call the police and Allison, well, she would just tell me not to talk to strangers."

Conny shook her head. "I can't believe it. Anyway, practically speaking..."

"I'm done being practical. I know the odds. I'm proud that I've been someone people could count on. But, I have never done a single thing in my whole life that wasn't—*sensible*." Her voice became shrill and loud.

Merry June moved the cake back in front of Conny and glanced at the guests on the floor clapping and gyrating to a local favorite, the *Chicken Dance*. "Maybe I'll get to see some movie stars when I'm there. I would give anything to see gorgeous George. Did you know…?"

"Your aunt Amy went to high school with his aunt Rosemary?" Conny finished for her. "Yes, I believe you may have told me that story once or twice." She grinned at her friend.

"How about if we tell Harold right now? I'll help you. I'll stand …"

"Behind me? No way. I know how that conversation would go and I'd end up caving in—like always."

"There's no way I can talk you out of it?"

Merry June shook her head.

"You'll call?"

"I'll let you know the minute I get there," Merry June said and checked her watch. "I have to leave for the airport now. I'm taking the red eye."

Conny chuckled. "Listen to you, you already sound like a movie star."

The women stood and embraced one last time. Merry June took a long white envelope from her purse.

"Will you give this to Harold for me?"

"Of course. What is it?"

"A note telling him what I've just told you." Merry

June's face lit up with an enormous smile of relief. "Also, directions for heating up the meals I left in the freezer, how to do the laundry, the phone numbers of all the service workers I could think of in case something goes wrong and," she shrugged, "what he needs to know just in case," she gulped, "in case something should happen to me."

"Merry June Pigg, that's horrible. Nothing bad is going to happen to you."

"Probably not. You know how I am though."

"He's going to be furious."

"I know. Thank goodness I'll be two thousand miles away."

FIVE

Merry June pushed and wiggled and sweated inside the bathroom stall. She was losing feeling in her thumbs hooked under the Spanx that refused to let go of her hips. She held her breath as she nudged the garment down one inch at a time until it landed around her ankles like a deflated whoopee cushion. She freed one high-heeled foot, then the other, smoothed the chiffon skirt of her dress into place and slid back the lock. *Freedom... nothin' left...* she sang under her breath.

She hurried through the lobby to the desk where she'd dropped her suitcases off earlier, gave the attendant her claim slips and asked for her luggage. She hoped none of her friends decided to leave the party early so she wouldn't have to make excuses about what she was doing. It was the weak link in her plan. Once she got to the airport, she'd change into the new velour tracksuit she'd packed in her carryon along with a month's supply of medications and a new pair of Nike's. She gave herself a mental pat on the back for her planning achievement.

I wonder what's taking so long? She peered around the desk into the luggage room. The bellman stood in the center of the room, scratching his head and staring at Merry June's claim stubs. He pushed a few pieces of luggage with his foot, compared the numbers on some bags like Merry June's and returned with just her backpack. Merry June's stomach knotted up.

"What's the matter?" Her voice was shrill even to her own ears. "Where's my other suitcase?" She snatched the bag from the young man.

"I cannot find it, Madame," he said in an accent Merry June didn't recognize. "Can you describe it for me, please?"

"It's black. It's a TravelPro, about this size." She moved her hands to illustrate.

"Can you please step inside and tell me if you see it?"

Merry June followed him into the luggage room that was filled with black suitcases similar to hers. The bellman pulled out one piece of luggage after another for her to examine.

She shook her head at each one. "Where's the woman who was here earlier?"

"That was Eloise. She was just filling in while I had my dinner. She's gone home for the day."

"She said she'd have my bags set aside for me when I came back. Maybe she put them on a special shelf or something?" Merry June was becoming increasingly agitated. "Mine had a red bow on it," she told him. "That should help." It narrowed the search down to two bags, identical to Merry June's down to the red bow. Neither one was hers.

"I must get my manager," the man said. "You wait here, please."

Merry June spotted her neighbors, Gayle and Rick, exiting the elevator and walking toward the main entrance. She ducked back into the luggage room and hoped they hadn't seen her. She breathed a deep sigh of relief when they walked outside to their Prius.

The bellman returned with an older man who introduced himself as Jacob, the Bell Captain.

"Ramon tells me there is a problem with your bag, um, Miss?" he said.

"Mrs., uh, Miss—Miss Wedding," Merry June said, using her maiden name and the one she had put on her application to the show. She'd thought it suited her possible contestant status better than Merry June Pigg.

"I'm very sorry to tell you that it looks like your bag was given to another customer by mistake. The man on duty yesterday, when you brought your bag in, is new to the job. I assure you, this kind of mistake..."

"But I must have my bag," Merry June interrupted. She was as close to a meltdown as she had ever been in her whole life. "My plane ticket, my money, my credit card." She began to cry. "Everything is in that bag."

Ramon looked close to tears too while Jacob put his arm around Merry June's waist and led her into his office and out of view of the other guests who had stopped to stare. He helped her into a folding chair pushed into the corner of the tiny office and instructed Ramon to return to his station.

"Miss Wedding. What a pretty name," he soothed while Merry June, despite her predicament, was too polite not to smile and blush.

Jacob took a starched, white handkerchief from his pocket and dabbed the tears from Merry June's cheeks. "There now, don't cry. It makes your face all blotchy and detracts from that beautiful smile."

She blushed some more and flashed her newly bleached teeth at Jacob.

"Isn't that better, Miss Wedding?"

"Merry June, please, Jacob," she said, with only the slightest hesitation.

"Okay, Merry June. Now what will no doubt happen is that the person who received your bag by mistake will come back as soon as they discover the error. I will call you the minute your bag is returned. Okay?"

Merry June began crying again with gusto. "My plane leaves in two hours," she wailed. "I can't wait." She leaned across the desk, grabbed Jacob's hands in hers, and clutched them against her breast, now very close to being exposed. Her hair, teased, sculpted and sprayed cement-like into place was becoming unglued and coils of gray ringlets sprang around her face.

"Oh, dear," Jacob said, "I have to speak with my supervisor." He placed Merry June's hands in her lap and glanced once at the breast now completely unleashed from her low-cut dress before he left the room.

"Yikes." Merry June followed his glance and realized she had become completely undone. She tucked in her chest, patted her hair hopelessly against her head and smoothed her skirt over her knees. When Jacob returned with his supervisor, she had regained some of her composure.

The supervisor took the seat behind the desk while Jacob stood behind him.

"I understand there's been a mix-up with your bag, Miss Wedding?"

Merry June nodded. She thought she detected a curling of the supervisor's lips.

"I believe Jacob explained that when your bag is returned, we will notify you. At that time, if you cannot come in and pick up the bag, we will be happy to ship it to you—at our expense of course," he added, before Merry June could interrupt.

"But my plane ticket is in that bag." She looked at her watch. "What am I going to do? My trip, the audition, all my planning? Everything will be ruined."

The supervisor shrugged as he got up to leave. "I'm sorry, Miss Wedding. It is never a good idea to leave valuables like that. We are not responsible—see, it says so on the back of your claim stub." He pointed to print so small Merry June couldn't possibly read it.

"I'll have to take your word for it," she said grimly.

He opened the door and offered her his hand. "Good night, Miss Wedding. Have a pleasant trip."

It was nearly eleven-thirty and the party would be breaking up soon. She went back to the Ladies' room and ducked into a stall so she could think about her predicament without being seen.

"Maybe this is a sign," she said to herself. "Maybe this was never meant to be." She took a long breath of air and shook her curls. *Pull yourself together and stop acting like a big baby.* It had been a pipe dream, the ideations of a silly old woman. *Whatever made me think I could manage a trip clear across the country? A grown woman who had never even been on a plane much less anywhere as exotic as California?*

And then there was the show itself—the most popular game show on television! She'd known from the start the odds were against her. She'd read that out of more than ten thousand hopefuls, only six hundred got picked to be on the show. It was just that she'd put all her misgivings out of her mind and focused on the planning and saving and what she would wear and how she would smile at the camera and mention Noah... *What did I say to Conny about being the practical one? That's a joke. It's time to go back. Maybe no one has missed me yet.*

She pulled herself up and put her hand on the lock. She tried to shut out images of the palm tree-lined

31

boulevards, red carpet nights, and stars in evening gowns and sparkling jewels that paraded through her mind's eye. When she opened her purse and pulled out a tissue, Harold's card fell out and landed next to her foot.

I forgot about this. She opened the card to a picture of two old people sitting on a park bench. Inside were the words, 'Happy Birthday' over Harold's signature. Merry June took a sharp breath when she saw that the card contained five crisp one-hundred-dollar bills.

"Holy moley," she said aloud. She fingered the bills. She started to laugh so hard she had to hold her sides and this time the tears were from the belly laughs that just kept on coming. "Oh my gosh. Harold, you don't know it yet, but you have just stopped me from flushing my dream down the toilet. Look out, Hollywood, Merry June Wedding is back on track."

SIX

Merry June changed into her tracksuit and sneakers. She folded up her dress and put it with her pumps into her backpack. Since the rest of her clothes were gone with the lost bag, the dress would have to be her backup.

That's better. She wiggled her hips and turned around. *Now, I need a plan.* She leaned against the stall door and fingered the money. *Hitchhiking is out of the question, or at least it's a last resort. A bus? I wonder how much a ticket clear across the country costs? Let's go and find out.* She adjusted the straps of her backpack and started to feel better now that she had a plan. She slipped three of the bills into her bra and the rest she divided up—one in each shoe. *Fool me twice...*

She put on fresh lipstick, ran a comb through her hair and repeated her hand washing routine twice instead of the requisite three times. *Let's get this show on the road.*

She dashed through the lobby and out the door, where she signaled a taxi before the hotel doorman could raise his whistle to his lips. Merry June jumped in the back seat and commanded the driver to take her to the bus station.

"Hurry, please." The trip took less than five minutes and when she handed him a hundred-dollar bill, the driver grumbled but managed to come up with the correct change minus a five-dollar tip for himself.

...

Bars, tattoo parlors, and graffiti- covered high-rise apartments surround the bus station located on the fringe of the city. Merry June hurried past a man slumped next to the door. He had one hand on a grocery cart brimming over with plastic garbage bags and growled at her under his breath when she passed by.

She winced when she stepped inside the crowded waiting room. Overhead fluorescent lights cast a jaundiced glow over long wooden benches. Families with infants in arms, sullen teenagers and haggard-faced parents sat crushed beside young men in battle fatigues. Others dozed against a rumble of whispered conversations and the rustle of bodies shifting on the hard seats.

Merry June stepped over outstretched legs and bags as she wound her way to the ticket window.

"I want to buy a ticket to Los Angeles," she told the woman behind the barred window.

"One-way, round trip, pass or senior?" the ticket seller yawned back at Merry June.

"One way, please. Senior," she added.

The woman drank from something swaddled in brown paper.

How much is it?" Merry June asked.

"With senior discount, one o five."

"Oh, gosh." She counted out the bills and noticed how fast her money was disappearing.

The woman pushed a paper ticket through the opening in the window. "You need to get the bus to L.A out of Chicago."

"I'm sorry?" Merry June said, stepping back to the window.

"I said, to get to L.A., first you have to go to Chicago. We ain't got no direct line to California from here. You wanna ticket to Chi-town?"

"I guess so," Merry June stammered. "How much is that?"

"One way or round trip? Pass or senior?"

"Definitely one way. Still senior," she scoffed. She was tired and out of sorts.

"That'll be forty-six dollars."

She looked at the shrinking wad of cash thinking she hadn't even left Cincinnati yet and had already spent a lot of money.

"What time...?"

"Bus leaves at one. Gets to Chi-town at six."

Merry June counted out the money, took the ticket and her change and looked for someplace to sit. She was worn out and hungry and realized she hadn't eaten anything at the party except cake and champagne. She spotted a vending machine in the corner but when she climbed over her fellow travelers, she saw a dog-eared, graffiti-ridden sign that read 'out of order'.

On the other side of the room, she spotted metal stools with red plastic tops, cracked and peeling, lined up along a counter. *At least it's a place to sit.* She squeezed onto a stool beside an elderly woman in a long, dirty wool coat, and a blue ski cap pulled over her face. The woman spoke animatedly and gestured as she talked. "Excuse me?" Merry June said, leaning closer. The woman responded by pulling the collar of her coat up around her ears and swiveling her stool so her back was to Merry

June.

"Ready to order?" A skinny waitress with blonde hair piled up at least six inches high, set her cigarette on the counter ledge and removed a pencil from behind her ear. She reminded Merry June of one of the waitresses from an old TV sitcom. The plastic nametag pinned to her collar read 'Sandi'.

Well, kiss my grits.

"You gotta order somethin' if you're gonna sit here," Sandi said. "If you ain't, then move outta the way for the payin' customers." She picked up her cigarette, took a long drag, and blew smoke in Merry June's direction.

Merry June stifled a fit of coughing and sputtered, "No, I am, going to order, I mean." She studied the greasy menu. "Coffee, please and um, a cheeseburger?"

"Gotcha," the waitress rasped. She set a glass of water in front of Merry June and headed for the kitchen.

"Um, Miss?" Merry June called out.

Sandi glanced back over her shoulder.

"Where's the Ladies room?"

"Out of order."

"But I need to wash…"

She was already gone.

Merry June was wiping her hands with the napkin

she'd dipped into her glass of water when a young man with shoulder length hair sat down next to her. He wore a brightly colored tam and a backpack that extended above his head and down to his hips. He carried a beat-up guitar case that he placed carefully at his feet. He slid the backpack from his shoulders and rubbed the places where the straps had been. He stared at the menu for a long time before counting out a handful of coins. 'Flo', and Merry June could only think of her that way, reappeared to take the young man's order. She did an eye roll when he ordered coffee and a glass of water with lemon.

The man glanced at the woman in the ski mask and winked at Merry June before lifting the steaming coffee to his lips. He closed his eyes as he leaned his head back and allowed the hot liquid to slide down his throat, draining the cup in one swallow.

"Man, that's good." He held out his cup for a refill.

When the waitress brought the cheeseburger, Merry June made the mistake of lifting the withered bun to look at the thin grey patty attempting to hide under a blanket of orange goo and a pickle. A couple of potato chips wilted beside the burger. Merry June's stomach growled, and she told herself she couldn't afford to waste food or money given the current state of her finances.

She cut the sandwich in half, closed her eyes, held her breath and nibbled a bite. The man watched her out of the corner of his eye.

"I don't think I can eat all of this," Merry June said, swiveling her seat towards him. "Would you care for the other half?" She pushed the uneaten part of the burger and the chips to the side of the plate with her knife.

"Why, thank you, ma'm," he said, his eyes locked onto the offering.

"Here, then, I'll just use my saucer and you take the plate." She deftly removed her portion and pushed the rest in front of him. He made the sign of the cross before he bowed his head and whispered a few words before turning his attention to the food. He polished off the burger and chips and wiped his mouth on the paper napkin the waitress had slipped beside his plate when she refilled his coffee for the third time.

"I'm gonna hafta throw this pie out unless I can sell it tonight." Sandi held up a wedge of lemon meringue so big it hung over the sides of the plate. "Ten cents," she said, passing it under Merry June's nose. "Interested?"

"Want to share?" Merry June asked her new companion.

"Only if you let me buy." The light bounced off the gold in his front teeth when he grinned.

"Deal," she said.

"I'm Rufus." He extended his hand.

"Merry June." She took his hand in both of hers. "Very pleased to meet you."

The waitress brought an extra plate with the pie and Merry June cut a sliver for herself, passing the rest to her new friend.

"Well, that was good." He scraped a few remaining crumbs from the plate and reached over to wipe meringue from Merry June's upper lip. "Where're you headed, MJ?" He dipped the corner of the napkin in his water glass and rubbed a spot on her cheek.

MJ—she liked that. She thought that might be a good stage name—MJ Wedding.

Merry June told him she was on her way to Los Angeles to audition for her favorite game show and how her suitcase with her plane ticket and money had gotten lost and she'd been about to forget the whole thing but when she found the money in Harold's card, she took it as a sign to carry on. She told him about her seventieth birthday, about the party and Harold, her children and Noah, and how she hoped she'd get to see some celebrities, one George in particular, when she got to California.

When she paused to take a breath, she realized she'd been talking nonstop. "I'm so sorry. Here I've been bending your ear with my life story when you were only being polite. You must think I'm a kooky old lady," she said and stole a glance at the woman next to her who continued to carry on a lively conversation with someone only she could see.

"No need to apologize, MJ. You're a very interesting lady. Besides, I bet once Harold and your kids and especially Noah see you win a fortune on that show, they'll be so proud of you, nothing else will matter."

"I hope you're right, Rufus. You're very sweet. But, what about you? Where are you going?"

"My momma lives in Chicago and I'm going home to see her. I've been away a long time, MJ." A shadow passed over his face. "I've had a rough time and I just want to put it behind me."

"I understand."

Rufus chuckled, "And all I had to do to gain some insight was get a Ph.D. in Psychology." He scraped bits of pie off the plate.

This latest revelation surprised Merry June and she

blurted out, "But I assumed you were down on your luck," she stammered. "Oh, I'm sorry. But the way you counted out your change, ordering just coffee..." she looked at him, embarrassed.

"Oh, I am," he confessed. "I had a great job in Atlanta teaching at a university and playing with a band whenever we could get a gig. Pretty soon the band began to take off and as a result, I started missing my classes, showing up late or hung over—I was a mess. Even after I got fired from teaching, I thought I could handle it. After all, I was still 'the doctor'." His laugh was devoid of mirth. "I turned to prescription drugs and more alcohol, lost my girlfriend, and ran through all my savings. Hit bottom as they say. But thanks to some friends who refused to lend me any money or take any of my crap, I got into a program, got my shit—oh, I am so sorry, MJ. I mean, I got my act together and found out I had a gift for counseling other addicts. And I liked it. I was able to land a job at a community health center in Chicago, near my mom, so I'm going home."

"I think that's wonderful, Rufus. You should be proud."

He rested his chin in his hands. "You know, I really am. I only hope my momma will forgive me. I have a lot of making amends ahead of me."

"We all need forgiveness at times, Rufus," she said. She thought about Harold and her children back at the party. Right about now, Conny was handing them the letter she'd written and Noah was filling in the blanks. She hoped Rob wouldn't be too hard on him for keeping his grandma's secret. "I'm going to be asking some people I love for a great big boatload of forgiveness when I get back home."

Rufus laughed, his hair bobbing.

"This is your stopover on the way?"

"Yeah, and I was here for a wedding. My roommate from college got married and he asked me to play for the ceremony." He pointed to the guitar with his chin.

"So are you a Cincinnati Bearcat?" Merry June said.

"Sure am."

"Me too. And I was a teacher too—middle school. I quit when the kids came along but when they started school, I went back to teaching. Worked out great. Of course, when I was in college, girls didn't have many choices when it came to careers—teacher, nurse, secretary—that was pretty much it." She hesitated then asked, "Can I ask you something personal?"

"Not if you don't mind if I refuse to answer."

"Could I feel your hair?" Merry June became a little embarrassed but went on anyway. "It's just that I've never seen such beautiful braids."

"Dreadlocks," he smiled at her.

"They just look so pretty with the way you wove in those beads—I've never seen, uh, deadlocks decorated like that."

Rufus took off his hat and placed Merry June's hand on his hair. "What do you think?"

She ran her fingers down the length of one of the coils. "It feels soft, nice. Thank you."

The announcement came over the P.A. that their bus was ready for boarding. They counted out the correct change and Merry June left *Flo* a two-dollar tip.

"Time to go." Rufus took her hand and kissed it, bowing as he did so. "I hope you find everything you're looking for, MJ."

"I'm so glad I met you, Rufus. And you tell your momma that the second big hug she gives you is from MJ Wedding."

...

The two were separated as they joined the crowd lining up for the bus. Merry June's feet scarcely touched the pavement as the crowd surged toward the door taking her with them. She fell into a seat right behind the driver and lost sight of Rufus as he made his way toward the back.

Merry June was so tired she could barely keep her eyes open. She immediately started to doze off when a heavyset woman with a squirming toddler plopped into the seat next to her. The child wiggled out of her mother's arms into the aisle where an elderly lady collided with the little girl sending them both to the floor. The older woman picked up the bags she dropped in the scuffle, repositioned her purse and a golf umbrella that she placed strategically over her arm so that when she started back down the aisle, she managed to stab Merry June's seat mate in the thigh.

The result was an outpouring of profanity from both women until Merry June couldn't stand it any longer.

"Shut up!" she shouted. Her hand flew to her mouth. She couldn't believe it. She never in her life had told anyone to 'shut up' even though she'd thought it plenty of times. She'd punished her children when they said it and now she was yelling the forbidden words at total strangers on a bus of onlookers. She was humiliated. She scooted down in her seat as far as she could and tried to become invisible.

Kandy Witte

"You tell 'um, MJ," Rufus's familiar voice hollered from the rear of the bus.

The bus driver blew the horn and instructed everybody to "do as the lady says—shut up—and sit down," he added for emphasis. He turned off the interior lights, backed the bus out of the lot and headed for the interstate.

SEVEN

The bus was full. It was a half-hour before the shuffling, throat clearing and whispering quieted and the passengers settled down for the trip to Chicago. The woman next to her held her child on her wide lap and was snoring in no time. Merry June used her backpack as a pillow, placing it against the cool glass of the window. She closed her eyes and hoped to get a few hours' sleep. She felt someone watching her and opened one eye just wide enough to see the little girl sucking her thumb and staring at her through the dimly lit cabin.

She sat up and looked closer at the child. She was a plump little girl with straight, dirty blonde hair that looked as though it hadn't seen a brush for quite a while. Her dress was several sizes too big, and she wore scuffed white sneakers with heels that flashed pink neon when she kicked them against the bus driver's seat. But none of those things mattered when Merry June looked into the child's eyes. They were big and so brown they were almost black. Thick, curling black lashes set off her look that was intelligent and wise beyond her years.

"You need to go to sleep," she told the child.

The girl sucked loudly and shook her head.

"Why not?"

"You might eat me up," came the reply.

"I will eat you up if you don't." Merry June was tired and cranky and she hadn't washed her hands right even once since she'd begun her adventure. She tried a different angle. "What's your name?"

"I ain't supposed to talk to strangers."

"That's true." She shut her eyes then sneaked a peek at the little girl who continued to stare back. "If I tell you my name, will you tell me yours? Then we won't be strangers. Besides, your momma's right here."

The child thought about that and patted her mother's cheek. "Momma? Can I tell the mean lady my name?"

Her mother snuffled an answer that might have been a 'yes'.

"I am not mean," Merry June said. "Your momma was yelling and I needed to make her stop. Now, you can tell me your name or not because I am going to sleep, and so

48

should you." Merry June repositioned her makeshift pillow against the window. She could feel the child's eyes on her but was determined to ignore her and force herself to get some rest.

A wet thumb poked Merry June's cheek. "You sleepin' yet?"

Merry June pretended to snore.

"I know you ain't sleepin'."

"Am so."

"Nu uh."

"Uh huh."

"Gigi."

"What?" Merry June opened one eye.

"I'm Gigi."

"Oh. I'm Merry June."

"That's a funny name. I gots a middle name too. And a last name. Gigi is my first name, Madrid, that's my middle name, and..."

"Hold on." Merry June sat up. "Your middle name is Madrid?"

"Yeah."

"That's unusual."

"Yeah. My last name's Espanola. My momma says I gots a pretty name 'cause I'm a pretty little girl."

49

"Gigi Madrid Espanola?" Merry June repeated. "Wow."

Gigi stretched out a tiny hand and squeezed Merry June's nose.

"Ow, stop that," Merry June said, taking Gigi's hand in her own. "Are you and your momma on your way home?"

"No."

"Are you going to visit somebody?"

Gigi put her thumb back in her mouth and sucked. She laid her head back on her mother's chest.

Merry June watched the little girl who watched back from under her long lashes. A small frown came and went around the tiny mouth as Gigi sucked harder on her thumb. She curled into a tiny ball on her mother's lap and buried her face in her mother's bosom. Merry June took off her jacket and laid it over the child. She brushed back a string of hair behind Gigi's ear and whispered, "Sleep tight."

...

The lights from the rest area in the first stop outside Indianapolis woke Merry June from her light sleep. Passengers stirred awake and many got off to stretch their legs or get snacks from the vending machines. Merry June ran a comb through her hair and put on lipstick to make herself feel better.

Gigi's mother squeezed out from beneath the sleeping child, yawned and spread her arms in a long stretch. "Would you mind watching her for me while I run to the Ladies?" she asked Merry June.

"I'd be glad to." Merry June felt even guiltier for telling the woman to "shut up" earlier. Traveling with a small child would try anyone's patience. It had tried hers and she had no responsibility to anyone but herself.

The woman lifted a plastic bag down from the overhead bin and moved heavily down the steps into the yellow light of the rest area. Some of the other passengers gathered in knots to smoke and exchange small talk. After several minutes, the driver returned and started up the engine. He turned on the heater and Merry June shivered when the warm air blew from the vent above her head.

"Thanks," she said leaning over the driver's seat. "That feels good. I was getting chilled."

He did a half turn in his seat and glanced at the sleeping child.

"Those two are regulars on this line," he told her. "They go to Chicago, then get right back on the bus and go back to Cincinnati. Sometimes they take the Cincy to Lexington bus then turn around and do the whole thing over again. The only time they take a break is the first of the month when mom gets her AFDC check, buys another thirty-day pass and off they go."

"They don't have a home, a family?" Merry June was incredulous.

"Not that any of the drivers know of. Mom's real closed mouthed, don't say much, but the scuttlebutt is that she's on the run from the kid's father. She told one of the other drivers that the guy beat her up so bad she landed in the hospital. He nabbed the girl and was halfway to Florida before the cops caught him thanks to an Amber alert and an observant civilian."

"That's horrible. But," she paused a minute so her voice wouldn't crack, "isn't the father in jail?"

"Naw, he got let go. Overcrowding or some such bullshit. So, they keep on ridin'."

Merry June was still trying to wrap her brain around the idea that Gigi virtually lived on a bus and the idea of these two riding day in and day out with no friends, no home, afraid for their lives, was unbearable.

"I feel bad now for yelling at her earlier," Merry June said.

"You did the right thing. Mom has a bad temper but I've never seen her take it out on the kid. Guess she's got it tough, being on her own and always havin' to look over her shoulder no doubt takes its toll." The driver shrugged. "Some of us drivers try to help out. We bring in clothes, toys, stuff our own kids or grandkids have outgrown. It's not much but..."

Merry June reached up and squeezed his arm. "But, it is."

"I guess it's something." He turned in his seat and flashed the headlights to signal the stragglers that it was time to go.

Gigi's mother returned and looked down at her sleeping daughter. Before she could pick up the little girl, Merry June held out her hands.

"Would you let me hold her for a little while? It's been a long time since I've had the chance to hold a little one. My last baby—my grandson, Noah, is a teenager now. I sure miss this." It was her way of apologizing for the earlier incident.

"I dunno."

"Traveling is stressful enough and with a child? I remember."

"Well, I guess it'd be okay. Just for a couple minutes."

Merry June gently slid her hands underneath Gigi's small body and shifted the child onto her lap. Gigi stirred

53

before falling back into a deep sleep.

"Wish I could sleep that soundly," Merry June said. She pulled her jacket snugly around the little girl.

"I'm getting better at it," said Gigi's mother. "By the way, my name's Aretha."

"Nice to meet you, Aretha. I'm Merry June."

Aretha opened a bag of potato chips she'd bought at the rest stop. She held out the bag, "Like some?"

"Thanks, but I had a lot to eat earlier tonight at the bus station."

"That food'll kill ya'," said Aretha, popping the top on a Coke.

The women rode in silence as Aretha finished what Merry June guessed was probably her dinner. She slipped off her shoes and leaned her seat back the standard two inches that airlines and buses alike call reclined.

"I'm wide awake now," Merry June lied. "If you want to take a nap, go right ahead. I'll let you know if Gigi wakes up."

"I guess it would be okay," Aretha said, obviously torn between handing her child over to a stranger on a bus and the exhaustion that was clearly overtaking her.

"She's out like a light," Merry June said. "She won't even know."

"Maybe just a short one, but..." Aretha's eyes shut before she got all the words out.

Merry June told Aretha the truth when she'd said she missed having little ones around. Rob and Allison had been only eighteen months apart and at the time, when Merry June wasn't changing or washing diapers—that was before disposables—she was sterilizing bottles, ironing Harold's shirts and trying to keep up with housework, grocery shopping, cooking. She couldn't remember ever having a date night with her husband like young couples did today. Managing a budget on Harold's salary alone had been challenging to say the least and extravagances like dinner out or movies were sacrificed for the kids having a stay-at-home mom during their preschool years. They had both agreed that she would postpone going back to teaching until the children were in school. It was a decision she never regretted and looking back, she thought it had gone by way too fast.

Merry June watched through the dirty window as the bus joined the cars and trucks flying past them on either side. Her thoughts drifted to Harold and the kids. She imagined Harold reacting to the news of her disappearance and Noah trying to explain her behavior to his dad. Her stomach clenched as she imagined their reaction. *Oh my God. What on earth have I done?*

...

The sky had faded from black to gray by the time they turned onto the exit ramp into the heart of the city. A train rattled by on the overhead rails and as the bus made its way through the labyrinth of the city streets. Giant skyscrapers, like soldiers standing at attention, blocked the sky creating the illusion that the daylight cycle was reduced to mere seconds and night had fallen again.

The driver steered the bus into a loading dock and turned on the interior lights to rouse the passengers including Aretha and Gigi. The child looked startled to find herself on Merry June's lap and reached her arms out to Aretha, her small mouth puckered as she prepared to cry. Merry June handed her back to her mother and as Aretha gathered the plastic grocery bags that held their belongings, Merry June took back her jacket and slung her backpack over her shoulder. The women said their goodbyes and Aretha hoisted her daughter onto her hip.

"Bye, Gigi."

The little girl blew her a kiss as her mother carried her down the steps and they disappeared into the crowd.

EIGHT

Merry June felt a light tap on her shoulder.

Rufus smiled down at her. "What time's your next bus?"

She looked around the large, crowded station. "Gosh, I don't know."

He took her elbow and steered her through the crowd. "Let's make sure you're all set."

Long lines of travelers crawled toward the ticket windows. Children clung to their mothers, elderly couples teetered on canes and walkers, young people with backpacks like the one Rufus wore, passed the time reading or texting on their smartphones.

Rufus kept a firm grip on Merry June's arm. He propelled her forward as one by one, travelers stepped up to a window and freshly ticketed, fanned out into the station with their interstate adventure secured in the palm of their hand.

Merry June's turn at the window finally came. She dug her ticket from her backpack and pushed it underneath the small opening toward the ticket seller.

"We want to know where her bus loads and what time," Rufus said through the glass.

The ticket seller entered some information into his computer and waited while the screen brought up columns of numbers and codes.

"Next available seats are tomorrow at three-thirty P.M," he said. "There are three seats left. Do you want to reserve one?"

"You mean there's nothing today? But I have a ticket." Merry June felt her stomach cramp in panic.

"Sorry. The earliest is tomorrow, three-thirty. You should have reserved a seat when you bought your ticket in Cincinnati. This ticket is for general seating. Reserve for tomorrow, three-thirty, or move on."

"I don't know. I guess so?" She looked to Rufus for help.

"Yes, she'll reserve a seat," Rufus told the man.

"That will be five dollars to reserve."

"Oh dear," Merry June said. "This is getting expensive." She took five singles from her wallet and passed them under the glass.

The agent exchanged her cash and traded the original ticket for the new one. He gave her the gate number and pointed to an escalator that would take her to the loading area. He warned her it was just like cash and if she lost it, she would have to buy another one. She nodded her understanding and put it into the fanny pack that she extracted from her backpack, buckled securely around her waist.

Rufus surveyed the crowded station with a frown. "Do you want me to help you find a hotel?"

"I'm on a really tight budget." He has no idea how tight, she thought. "I'll be fine here. There's a McDonald's, places to sit. I'll be fine—really," she said again and tried to sound a lot braver than she felt.

"I hate to leave you like this. Hold on a minute." He took out his cell phone and walked away to place his call.

He returned a few minutes later. "It's all set, you're coming home with me. That was my momma I called. She insisted." He grinned.

"That's sweet of you, both of you, but you've already done too much for me. I couldn't impose."

"It would be a favor to me, MJ. I could sure use some moral support when I face my momma again. I'm not sure how she's going to react. She'll probably open the door holding a frying pan to bash my head in. Not that I don't deserve it," he added.

Merry June hesitated a moment before she agreed. "Only if you allow me to pay the cab fare," she insisted.

"This is Chicago, MJ. We use the train."

...

During the short ride to his home, Rufus told her his mother's name was Shirley and she'd moved to the neighborhood after Rufus's father deserted the family. His mother, a high school Social Studies teacher, was a strict disciplinarian who made sure Rufus understood the value of education from a young age.

"She's the reason I got my doctorate. I wanted to make her proud. The other stuff," he paused, "that was all on me."

From the train station, Rufus led her to a neat, high-rise apartment building in an area that was a mix of more apartment buildings, single-family homes, and small businesses and restaurants.

"Momma even gave up her car. She said if she couldn't walk to a place or get there by bus or train, she didn't need to go there."

"Well, this is it." He took a deep breath and knocked.

Voices coming from a television inside went suddenly quiet. Heavy footsteps approached and the door swung open. A large woman in a beautiful blue silk dressing gown stood in the doorway and gazed up at her son. After a moment of looking him over from head to toe, a smile lit up her face as she flung open her arms and Rufus disappeared into her embrace. The two held on like they'd never let go.

When Shirley finally released her son, Rufus stepped back to introduce Merry June. "Momma, this is..."

He didn't get the words out before Shirley had Merry June in a hug that took her breath away. "Welcome to my home, MJ," she greeted her. "I'm so pleased you could come."

Shirley ushered them into a living room that was warm and elegant. Overstuffed sofas and chairs slipcovered in cream and pale blue provided a welcome sight to Merry June who was both physically and emotionally exhausted. French doors opened onto a wide balcony with a view of the city, the framework of the Ferris wheel at Navy Pier outlined in the distance and sailboats appearing like cotton balls drifted on the lake.

"Your home is lovely." Merry June suddenly felt very unsure of herself as it dawned on her that she had allowed herself to be persuaded to stay the night in the home of virtual strangers. She shuddered when she imagined Harold's reaction when she told him. He'd send adult protective services after her for sure.

"Show MJ to your old room, son, and where she can wash up," Shirley said all in one breath. "Then come on out here and we'll have some iced tea, and we can all catch up."

...

After a good night's sleep and a huge breakfast, it was time for Merry June to leave. As they said their goodbyes, Shirley insisted that she come back for a longer visit when she returned from California. "I know you'll pass that audition, no problem. And we'll be watching when you win that bag of gold." She grabbed Merry June for one last hug.

"I'll be back and next time dinner's on me. I want to try some of that famous Chicago pizza Rufus was bragging about," Merry June joked. "And I'll send you some of our Cincinnati-style chili."

Rufus insisted on accompanying Merry June back to the bus station, and despite her protests, she was grateful for his help.

"This is where I have to say goodbye, MJ," he told her

once they reached the station and located the loading platform for the bus to L.A. "Here's my card for when you come through again. I want to hear all about your adventure." He wrapped his strong arms around her.

"I'm so glad I met you," Merry June said, her eyes misty. "I wish you all the best, Rufus. You are a very special man, and," she paused, "I can see how proud your momma is of you."

She waved as she watched him disappear into the crowd. She felt very much alone and for the first time since her journey began, she was frightened. She shook off those thoughts, told herself she was being silly and headed toward a brightly lit area with some shops and a food court.

She splurged and bought a copy of *The Atlantic*. She promised to treat herself to a hot fudge sundae from the McDonald's dollar menu and found a seat next to a long wall that separated the food court and shops from the ticket counters. She flipped through her magazine but since it cost over eight of her precious dollars, she wanted to save it until she got on the bus so she wouldn't be tempted to buy another one. She was really worried about her money situation and prayed Jacob would have recovered her suitcase by now. If she just knew it had

63

been returned, she could breathe easier.

She bought the sundae and a senior coffee and settled down to wait. She had another five hours before the bus boarded at two forty-five. The sugar and caffeine helped to wake her up temporarily but now she felt exhaustion wash over her. She folded her hands across her stomach and over her fanny pack and leaned her head against the wall. I'll just close my eyes for a minute.

...

Merry June felt rough hands shaking her awake. "Go someplace else and do your sleeping, lady," a man's harsh voice yelled in her ear.

When she opened her eyes, she was confused. "Where am I? Who are you and why are you yelling at me?"

The man released his grasp. "Whatsa matter, lady? Is sometin' wrong wit ya?"

"What time is it?" Merry June said.

"It's a quarter to."

"Quarter of two?"

"Nah, it's quarter to twelve. They's people wantin' to eat lunch and they needs a place to sit. You're just settin' here sleepin but now you got to buy some food so's you ken set here or you got to move along."

Merry June was beginning to come to but was still groggy. "Where am I?"

"Lady, you're in the bus station, in Chicago," the man's voice changed from anger to concern. "Say, you don't look so good. Don't move, now, ya hear? I'll be right back. I'm gonna git you some help." He patted her shoulder self-consciously and trotted away, looking back over his shoulder to make sure she hadn't run off.

Merry June noticed her fanny pack as if for the first time and quickly went through the contents. She was relieved to find her money still there and unfolded the ticket stuck inside. "Los Angeles," she stared. "What am I thinking?"

The man who had awakened her showed up with another man in black trousers and a white shirt with the words 'Security' stitched on the pocket. He leaned over Merry June's face and spoke slowly, as though she were a small child or someone who didn't speak English. "Hi there." He stretched out the words and raised his voice in case, Merry June guessed, she was also hard of hearing.

"I understand there's a problem?" he said. It sounded like he was talking to her underwater.

By this time, Merry June was fully awake and in control of both her tongue and her brain. "There's no problem, officer," she smiled at him sweetly. "I simply fell asleep and was momentarily confused at being suddenly awakened. I apologize to you and to this kind gentleman for any distress I may have caused either of you. I hope you will forgive me."

The atmosphere changed as the men, clearly impressed by Merry June's little speech, became tongue-tied and embarrassed. Merry June held out her hand first to the guard and then to the other man and shook each one with a firm grip and a rather haughty smile.

"I believe I will follow this young man's advice," she inclined her chin toward the first man, not young by any stretch of the imagination, "and find something to eat. My bus boards shortly and I prefer to dine here as one never knows what one will find en route." Merry June was really enjoying her act now that she had decided on a persona. She envisioned herself as Queen Elizabeth in a conversation with her subjects.

"I don't know," muttered the guard, clearly uncertain as to what to do with this woman, wide-awake and obviously in control of herself.

"I am fine, I assure you," Merry June said rising. "Thank you so much for your kindness to a," she looked at her feet, a small smile playing around her lips, "woman of my, um, rather advanced age." She opened her blue eyes wide and looked at each man with the full bounty of her undivided attention.

The guard shrugged." I guess it's okay, lady. You be careful, you hear?"

She nodded solemnly and gave the men a thumb's up.

"Whew," Merry June said under her breath, "that was a close call." She located the restroom where she performed her hand washing ritual and waited for a fellow traveler to open the door so she could avoid touching the handle. She wandered through the crowd then killed some time browsing the shops, glancing at souvenir tee shirts and mugs, resisting the urge to buy anything.

She wandered over to the bay where her bus was scheduled to depart and squeezed onto a bench with other passengers. *I better call home.*

She retrieved her phone from the fanny pack and thought about what to tell them. I'll just let them know I'm fine and that there would be a slight delay in getting to Los Angeles. Merry June knew the call would start a fight, 'how could you', 'have you lost your mind' and more and frankly, she just didn't have the energy to get into all that right now. Noah had insisted on teaching her the text function on her phone before she left so she decided she would use that to tell him about her change of plans.

It took her ten minutes to write the brief message; 'Missed plane. Taking bus. L.A. Tuesday. Call u when I arrive. Tell Grandpa.' She hit the 'send' button when the announcement came over the loudspeaker that it was time to board. Merry June gathered up her few belongings, tightened her jaw, stiffened her back and strengthened her resolve.

NINE

As the ticket seller had told her, the bus was full and Merry June ended up sitting in the rear next to the restroom. It wasn't a great seat, but she decided to make the best of it and hoped the passengers would take advantage of the frequent rest stops rather than the onboard facilities. Her seatmate was a pleasant looking woman who spoke only Spanish and Merry June was relieved that she wouldn't have to feel obliged to make conversation. She was content to watch the miles of cornfields sweep past her window and thought, as she often did, the Midwest was the most beautiful place in the world. *Of course, I haven't been away from home except the time Harold and I went to Indy. Maybe I'll change my mind as we get further west.*

As she sat back and watched the scenery, her mind drifted to thoughts of home and her family and friends. *I wonder if Harold has gotten over the shock. He's not exactly a man who can handle even the smallest upsets in routine much less the big ones.* She put her hand over her mouth to stifle a laugh. She remembered the time she decided to celebrate a profitable afternoon with her Red Hat ladies at the Horseshoe Casino in Cincinnati by picking up Chinese for dinner on her way home. Harold made a big scene, refused to even try a bite of the moo goo gai pan and accused her of trying to poison him with sushi. He demanded that she make him something edible, so she fried him some bologna and ate her ruined meal in the bedroom alone where she spilled soy sauce on the bedspread. There were other times they'd argue over a new brand of toothpaste or when he'd complain because Costco moved his oatmeal to a different aisle. She'd always say in her best schoolteacher voice, "To quote Heraclitus, 'The only thing that is constant is change'" and Harold would always snap back, "You can try to teach a Pigg to dance, but it doesn't work, and it annoys the hell out of this Pigg."

She closed her eyes. *To say I'm in a rut is the understatement of the year, but I have tried to make some changes. What about when I asked Frieda to add that swath of pink to my bangs? That was pretty bold. Or,*

getting my tattoo? She'd been scared to death when she
found herself in the tattoo parlor at the mall and that first
pinch of the needle almost made her change her mind.
But, she admitted she was glad she went through with it
and whenever she pictured that tiny bag of gold, like the
one from *Fortune Hunt,* sitting on her hip, it always made
her smile.

…

At the thirty-minute rest stop in Des Moines, Merry June
got out to stretch her legs before joining the queue in the
long line for the women's restroom. A young woman,
dressed in skintight jeans and high top sneakers
announced she was going to use the men's restroom
pointing out that there was 'no line over there.' She
tugged at Merry June's sleeve and asked her to go with
her to guard the door. "Then I'll be the lookout for you,"
she said.

Merry June thought a minute, as she really had to go,
and was regretting the bottle of water she'd had at the
station. "Okay," she agreed and followed the young
woman to the other side of the building.

"You stand here," she said. She grasped Merry June by
the shoulders and positioned her in the middle of the
opening that led to the men's toilet. "What's your name?"

"Mer—just MJ," she answered figuring this was a good time to start using her 'new' name.

"Okay, MJ. I'm Sarah. Now, just stand right here. If anybody comes, stick your arms out and tell them it's temporarily out of order. Got it?" Sarah looked doubtful that Merry June was up for the job.

"Sure," said Merry June like she'd done this a million times. When one of the male passengers approached, Merry June said, "Sorry, out of order" just as Sarah came outside.

"Funny, lady," said the man to Merry June. He turned back to Sarah. "Wanna go back inside for some fun?"

"Tell it to your wife, moron," Sarah said.

He gave her the finger on his way inside and brushed past them a minute later on his way back to the bus.

"You next," Sarah said to Merry June.

"I'm not sure now," Merry June said, her confidence rattled.

"Go ahead, MJ." Sarah gave her a push and she was inside. She faced a row of urinals before she spotted a stall at the end of the room.

Merry June finished her business and went into her hand washing routine. She was on the second round, "I wash my hands all day long, I wash..." when Sarah poked her head around the corner.

"What the hell's taking you so long, MJ? The bus is ready to pull out."

"I'll be there in a minute. Can you tell him to wait?" Merry June was only halfway through her ritual.

Sarah came forward and taking Merry June by the arm steered her toward the door.

"But I didn't finish washing up," Merry June protested.

"Finish on the bus or you'll be walking to California," Sarah told her. She looked harder at Merry June, "You ever done this before? Been on a bus trip?"

"Once, Harold and I went with the senior citizens center to Indianapolis. We took a bus that time."

Sarah motioned for Merry June to step into the bus ahead of her. "Well, MJ, this kinda bus trip is different. You have to pay attention to the time at these rest stops, or you will be left behind. You didn't see the driver counting heads, did you?"

Merry June shook her head.

"And always keep an eye on your stuff," Sarah instructed. "Is that your backpack on the seat, MJ?"

"Yes, I thought..."

Sarah clucked her tongue and shook her head. "MJ,

the cardinal rule of bus riding is don't never, I mean, *never*, leave your stuff unattended."

"Oh, dear, do you think anybody would..."

"No, MJ, I don't think so, I know so. That's a fact. Considered yourself warned."

The bus backed up and the driver yelled, "Take your seats, ladies."

Sarah settled herself in her seat across the aisle from Merry June and went to sleep.

Merry June held her breath while she did a quick look through her backpack. Everything was there—this time, she thought with relief. She read her magazine, dozed, and watched the scenery until the bus pulled into a truck stop.

"Forty-five minutes," the driver announced. "Stragglers will be left." He waggled a finger at Merry June.

"Don't worry about me," she shot back. She pulled her backpack from the overhead, checked her watch and followed the others into the restaurant already crowded with truckers enjoying an evening meal. Merry June returned from washing her hands and found a stool at the long counter where she asked the waitress for a menu.

M$. FORTUNE

"You don't want to order off the menu," the man next to her said. He leaned over and took it from her.

"I don't?"

He shook his head. "Special, for the lady, Lou."

Lou jotted something down on her pad and stuck it on a clip with a bunch of other orders where an arm from the back reached through and grabbed them by the handful. The place was busy and things moved fast; orders came and dishes were cleared to make room for the constant wave of new customers. The line at the cashier's counter snaked around the tables where people ate, talked, laughed and scraped their chairs as they came and went. The noise level was loud and boisterous and the mood was festive.

"Thank you," Merry June said to the man. "By the way, what did I order?"

"Open-face roast beef with mashed potatoes, green beans and roll. Coffee and choice of apple or chocolate pie."

"That's a lot of food."

"Right," he swallowed a gulp of coffee, wiped some gravy off his chin and turned back to Merry June. "Name's Al." He held out a hand for Merry June to shake.

"MJ," she said taking his hand.

"What does MJ stand for?"

Merry June hadn't considered the idea that she would have to explain this but told him, "Merry June. But I'm trying out the MJ thing. For my stage name," she added, surprising herself.

"You an actress?" Al seemed startled.

"Not yet," she admitted. "But I am going to Hollywood to try to be one, an actress, I mean." Even to Merry June the whole thing seemed absurd when she said it out loud.

"Cool. Ever acted in anything before?"

Encouraged, Merry June said, "In high school I was Liesl in *The Sound of Music* and I did a few small parts in our community theatre before my kids were born. But I've always had the bug," she finished truthfully. "And my birthday is the thirtieth so this is my present to myself."

"Good for you, MJ," Al said. He checked his watch.

Merry June apologized for talking so much but Al said that wasn't it. "It's almost your birthday, MJ."

"Really?" She was shocked it had come up while she wasn't paying attention. "I guess I've had so much going on, I didn't realize..." She told Al about the party, Noah, and ended with her story of 'running away from home'. "And here I am," she said proudly, having convinced herself again that what she was doing was perfectly normal for a seventy-year-old woman with a husband, two grown kids and a grandson. She realized she was finally getting used to the idea herself.

"I think you've got moxie as my old man used to say. Real moxie." Al smiled.

MJ blushed.

"Over here, Lou," Al waved the waitress over and whispered something in her ear.

A few minutes later, Lou reappeared with a slice of chocolate pie with a candle burning in the center. Al stood up and whistled to get everyone's attention. "It's MJ's birthday, folks," he shouted over the din. "Let's sing her a round of 'Happy Birthday'." He started the song and everyone joined in ending with a resounding 'and many mooooore!' They all clapped before turning back to their food and conversations.

Merry June blew out the candle. "That was so sweet, Al." She was really touched.

Al sipped his coffee as he told her how he had been a trucker since he graduated from high school thirty years ago. He told her he loved being on the road and traveling around the country, but, he admitted, he missed his family and felt the job cost him his marriage. He said he also had two grown children, a boy and a girl. He looked sad when he talked about how seldom he saw them but said since the economy had gone downhill, his business, like everyone's, was suffering which meant more time at home.

"The funny part is now I have more time to spend with my kids, they have less time to spend with me." Al got out his wallet and showed Merry June pictures of his children sitting around a picnic table on either side of their dad. "That was taken over the Fourth of July," his voice cracked as he rubbed his thumb over the surface. "Sorry, I'm kind of an emotional guy."

Merry June opened her fanny pack to pay for her lunch, but Al stopped her, putting his hand over hers.

"My treat," he said.

"Oh no, I couldn't."

"Happy Birthday, MJ. See you in the movies." He laid some money on the counter and started for the door. He glanced outside then turned to Merry June who was right behind him. "Didn't you say you were on a bus trip?"

"Yes." Her heart skipped a beat.

"I don't see a bus out here. Where'd he park?"

"It was right by the door. Right there," Merry June's voice rose to a high pitch as she pushed past Al and looked around the parking lot and the empty spot where the bus had been. She checked her watch and couldn't believe it—she had lost track of time and an hour had come and gone. The bus had left without her. She was stranded again with hardly any money and less than halfway to her destination and her dream.

TEN

Merry June broke down right in the door of the restaurant. She couldn't believe it. *I'm a ridiculous old lady who doesn't even know what day it is much less the time.*

'This was a stupid idea and I'm stupid and I'm going to call Harold and tell him I'm an idiot and if he can find it in his heart to take me back, I'll go straight home." She cried and sobbed.

Al stood watching, occasionally patting her shoulder saying, "There, now, it'll be okay. Don't cry."

She cried harder.

Finally, she simply ran out of steam, the tears refused to fall anymore, and she heaved one last deep sigh and threw back her shoulders. She looked around at the small crowd that had gathered around her and waited to see what would happen next.

She could see Al looked as upset as she felt. She could still taste the cream from her 'birthday' pie and feel the weight of her sparkly pumps and her beautiful dress in her backpack. Then, she made a decision. "Tomorrow is my birthday," she said in the confident tone she'd been practicing for her audition, "and MJ Wedding is no quitter! I have decided to stay the course!" It was melodramatic but the people seemed to like it as they cheered and shouted, 'way to go MJ.' Al gave her a thumb's up and headed for the parking lot.

Then, she was alone.

"Maybe my bravado was a little premature," she said to the empty lot. She found a spot on a bench just outside the front door and sat down to think. She was sending off a text message to Noah when a semi-truck pulled up to the door and the driver blew the horn. Merry June squinted into the cab where Al waved and motioned for her to get in. She walked around to the driver's side.

"Climb in. Maybe we can catch up with your bus. I have to get this load to Grand Island—that's on your route."

"I can't ask you to do this." Merry June's hopes rose but she was reluctant to take up his offer.

"You didn't ask me, I asked you. Besides, I feel responsible for making you lose track of time. And, I would sure enjoy the company. It gets awfully lonely out here and you're a nice lady. What do you say, MJ?"

"Well, if you're sure. You won't get in trouble, will you? I mean is this allowed? A passenger, I mean?"

"No problem." He seemed a little evasive.

Merry June retrieved her backpack and Al came around to the passenger's door to give her a boost up onto the seat. She buckled her seatbelt and they started off.

"This is a neat view from up here," Merry June observed. "You can see right into people's cars and everything."

Al chuckled. "You'd be surprised the things I've seen. People do more things in a car driving ninety miles an hour down the road than I've done on any honeymoon with one of my wives."

"One of?"

"Oh, didn't I mention that I had three wives? One at a time of course."

"Your children?"

"My first marriage, the only one that really counts. The love of my life, MJ. The other two, well, they were nice girls. Deserved a lot better than me. I was on the rebound, trying to get over Rhonda dumping me, and just kept getting married. Real sorry I hurt those ladies."

"Do you ever hear from Rhonda?"

"Oh, sure. We found out we're better at being exes than being a couple. I spend the holidays with her and the kids when I can. I get along with Bert, too."

"Bert?'

"That's the guy she married after me. He's a good husband and a great father to my kids. I like him. And he comes home every night. He's a mechanic for Delta Airlines so he makes good money. At least he did until Delta downsized in Cincinnati. Last I heard he was being laid off. This recession—I think it's a depression—is killing hard working families all over this country. Damn politicians. Both parties."

Al looked over at Merry June. "You doin' okay?"

"Fine, thanks. This is really fun."

"Uh oh."

"What, what's the matter?" Merry June sat up and looked down the road.

"We're coming up on a weigh station."

"Am I putting you over?"

"What?"

"Am I making you be overweight?" Merry June worried.

"No, that's not it." Al laughed. "But remember when you asked me if I could get into trouble for having a passenger?"

"Yes."

"Well, the truth is, I'm really not supposed to. Usually when I get to this weigh station, it's closed, but I'm later than normal today and I'm going to have to go through an inspection."

"I can explain what happened." Merry June was frightened. The last thing she wanted was to get Al into trouble. "What will they do to you?"

"Probably just a fine." He tried to sound casual, but he looked worried.

Merry June looked over the back of her seat. "What's back there?"

"My living quarters, bed, TV, fridge."

"Do they check there?"

"Not usually. What are you thinking?"

"Well, I could climb back there and get into your bed. If anybody finds me, I'll say I sneaked into your truck while you were at the truck stop. I'll tell them I missed my bus and saw a chance to catch a ride and a little shuteye. You had no idea I was back here." Merry June looked pleased with herself and decided she could be very convincing if the need arose.

"You're a great actor, MJ." Al chuckled. "Okay then," he pulled aside the drape that separated the cab from the sleeping quarter. "Do your thing."

"Nitey-nite, Al." She pulled back the covers and snuggled into the narrow but comfortable bed. She pulled the drape closed and listened to the hum of the wheels and lulled by the movement of the truck, she fell asleep.

...

When she woke up, she didn't know where she was. It was pitch dark with the only light coming from lampposts around a parking lot and headlights flashing past on the highway. It was quiet except for the sounds of vehicles humming in the distance. She peeked through the curtain and saw Al lying across the front seat of the cab. His legs were bent to accommodate his long frame, his worn cotton jacket was pulled up to his chin like a short blanket and his Cincinnati Reds baseball cap was pulled down over his eyes.

She realized they were parked at a rest stop on some interstate highway, but she had no idea where. She needed to use the restroom but didn't know how to get

85

past Al without waking him up, so she lay back down and got out her cell phone. There were only two bars left and she wondered how she would charge the battery. Her cell was her only link with Noah and therefore her family.

She checked her Inbox and saw three messages. The first one was from Allison demanding to know how Merry June could have done this to them and that they had been worried sick. Allison cautioned her mother to 'be careful, have fun and get George's autograph when you see him.' She closed with her usual warning, "don't talk to strangers." That made Merry June laugh. If she only knew.

She sighed and opened the text from Rob. Might as well get this over with, she thought as she considered her eldest child; quiet, cautious, and adverse to risk-taking—like his father. Rob was a gentle man and kind, a great dad but he could be stubborn, Merry June admitted to herself. She confessed that she might have been part of the reason he'd inherited that particular trait.

"Come home—now!" was the opening line of Rob's message followed by the reassurance that 'everything's fine.' He went on to ask if she wanted him to wire her money somewhere and to call dad ASAP.' *Yeah, right. Like that'll happen.*

The last text was from Noah telling her everybody had been in an uproar at first but were starting to get used to the idea. Harold relaxed when he read her letter telling him she had prepared thirty homemade meals for him that he would find in the garage freezer, each labeled with cooking directions. In addition, he appreciated the new underwear and socks that should last him until she returned, eliminating the need for him to do laundry if he was careful.

In addition, Merry June had paid all the bills two months ahead, taken the cat to the vet for a checkup, had both the Honda's serviced and done anything else she could think of to make this as easy on her husband as possible. The only thing she had not done was to listen to that voice in her head that repeated, *you can't be serious. Settle down and act your age.*

ELEVEN

She sat up and looked outside. A truck pulled into the spot next to theirs and shut off the lights but left the engine running. The driver climbed down and went into the building. He returned a few minutes later with a woman who, from what Merry June could make out in the dim light, looked to be in her late twenties. She wore a black miniskirt and a low-cut red sweater that left little to the imagination. Her black, patent leather boots reached mid-thigh and her bright red hair bounced around a pretty, if careworn, face. She climbed into the passenger's side of the truck and the driver followed behind her. A hand reached out to draw a black curtain around the side windows and the truck's windshield.

"Hmmm, interesting," Merry June said out loud.

Al mumbled something and stirred. He stretched his legs out straight one at a time as he started to wake up.

"I'm sorry. I didn't mean to wake you."

"S'okay," he said sitting up and rubbing his eyes. "You were really sawin' logs."

"I feel terrible about taking your bed."

"No worries. I've learned to sleep anywhere, through anything."

"How did it go at the weigh station?"

"No problem. I sorta wanted to see you do your act if they found you though. That woulda been fun." His deep laugh reminded her of Harold's when something really tickled him. She felt a twinge of homesickness at the thought.

"I'm not sure fun is how I'd describe it."

Al sat up and put on his cap. "Do you need to go inside?"

"I do that." Merry June found her backpack and climbed into the front. "Be right back."

...

Merry June was at the sink, brushing hair that reminded her of the time her grandmother had gotten a bad perm. Her curls stood straight out like short, fat gray swimmers getting ready for the high dive except on the right side where she'd slept, they lay flattened against her head. Merry June brushed and combed, held her head under the facet and even wet, her hair had the same lopsided look.

"What the heck," she was saying to her reflection when the woman in the black miniskirt walked inside. Merry June said, 'hello' and refused to let her mind go where it wanted to, reminding herself that appearances didn't matter. Just one look at herself, wrinkled, disheveled, no makeup, was enough to put that notion to rest.

She was finishing her hand washing routine when the woman came out of a stall and took the sink next to Merry June's. She looked at Merry June in the mirror and flashed a big smile.

"Hi," she said.

"Hi," said Merry June.

"I'm a wreck," the woman said, as she applied fresh mascara and lipstick.

"I should be such a wreck," Merry June smiled back. "You look great. I love your boots," she said, really meaning it.

"Why thank you, sugar. That's sweet."

"Can I ask you something?" Merry June said slowly.

"Well, I don't know. What is it?"

"This is going to sound peculiar, but..."

"Oh, just spit it out, lady." Her voice turned gruff, and she yanked her comb hard through her red curls.

"Well," Merry June was afraid to go on now, but she forged ahead anyway. "I missed my bus back a ways and got a ride with Al, that nice young man in the black and yellow truck out there, and I had to hide in the bunk at the weigh station and I fell asleep and I woke up, here." She paused to catch her breath. "I didn't, I mean I don't, know where we are. I'm supposed to be in California by now and my money got lost and oh, dear, everything is such a mess." She threw up her hands in exasperation.

The woman put down her comb and hugged Merry June.

"Oh, sugar," she said in a sweet drawl, "I'm sorry. I didn't mean to be rude, I just thought...well, sug, it doesn't matter. Now, first off, we're in Grand Island, Nebraska and it's Tuesday."

"Tuesday?" Merry June couldn't believe it. "Tuesday? Are you sure?"

"Well just turning Tuesday. About four in the morning, sug. Is there somethin' the matter with Tuesday?"

"Sort of," said Merry June. "It's just that my birthday, my seventieth birthday, was the 30th, Monday."

"No, it isn't," said the red haired woman.

"I guess I know when my own birthday is," Merry June snapped. "I may be a senior citizen, but I haven't lost all of my marbles—not yet anyway." She was indignant. Old people get such a bad rap.

"No," said the woman laughing, "I mean today is the thirtieth. That makes today your birthday."

"Really? Oh, dear. I really am losing it. Must be the birthday turned me senile."

"I don't know about that, but I sure needed a good laugh," said the woman. "Thanks, sug."

Merry June held out her hand and the woman took it in both of hers. "I'm Merry June but I go by MJ. MJ Wedding," she added as an afterthought.

"What a pretty name, MJ. It's nice to meet you. I'm Sally."

"MJ?" Al called from the entranceway, "You okay?"

"I'm sorry, Al. I'm fine," she called back. "I'll be right there."

"That's the kind driver who gave me a lift," she told Sally. "Come outside, I want you to meet him." She took Sally's hand and led her to the rig where Al stood chatting with the driver of the truck she had seen Sally with before.

Both men looked shocked as Merry June introduced Sally to Al. The other driver was red-faced and didn't say anything but climbed into his rig and pulled away.

"I guess I better get going too," Sally said. "I'm leaving this hick town tonight and I'm never comin' back."

"Where you going?" Al said.

"Vegas," said Sally. "I hear a girl can make a lot of money there. I want to be a dealer, but," she paused, "I'll probably have to be a waitress, or something, first." She made a face when she said the 'or something'.

"Well, isn't that interesting," Al said. Merry June said she thought so too.

"MJ here is on her way to L.A. to be on television.

"Wow, that's very cool, MJ."

"Sally, I wonder if you could help me and MJ out?"

"Sure, if I can."

Al turned to both women who waited expectantly. "Pretty soon, I'll be dropping my load off in town. Then, I'll pick up another one to haul back to Chicago." He coughed and rubbed the heel of his boot over a cigarette butt in the gravel. "What I'm saying, MJ, is this is as far as I go and I was thinking," he turned to Sally, "that if you're going to Vegas, and that's on MJ's way to L.A., maybe you wouldn't mind giving her a lift?"

"Oh, I couldn't impose." Merry June felt like the old maid aunt who got passed around to the various relations at Christmas and Thanksgiving. "If you could just drop me off in town, Al, I'll have my son wire me some money and catch a bus back home. I appreciate your kindness more than I can say, I really do, but this whole trip has been jinxed from the start. It's time for me to face the truth. I'm a silly old woman who thought she could live out some pipe dream. I've been nothing but trouble to my family, my friends and now to you nice people." She shrugged. "I took my shot. It didn't work out like I'd hoped, but at least I can say I tried."

Sally didn't say anything. Al looked sad but relieved. Neither tried to talk her out of her plan to return home.

Sally turned and gave Merry June a goodbye hug. "It was real nice to meet you, MJ," she said, "I'm sure sorry your plans didn't work out.

"I'm just going to run back inside for a minute and take one more stab at making myself presentable," said Merry June. Al walked Sally over to a beat-up Ford Fiesta and stood there talking while they waited.

Merry June returned looking the same and all three said their goodbyes again. Al and Merry June waved to Sally who peeled out onto the highway ahead of them. It was five a.m. when they got to the city limits. Al told MJ he'd drop her off at a truck stop with a Western Union office where Rob could wire her the money to go home.

"Guess this is it," Al said, handing down her backpack from his seat in the truck.

Merry June had insisted he go on to get back on schedule. They'd already exchanged phone numbers and email addresses and both were thinking of the roads ahead.

TWELVE

The Western Union counter didn't open for another two hours so Merry June went to the restroom, repeated her hand washing routine four times to make up for the times she'd missed and found a seat by the window. She decided to splurge and ordered the 'Road Warrior's Breakfast' since her adventure was coming to an end. In another two days, she'd be back at home, fixing Harold's dinner, cleaning, running errands—all the usual activities of a humdrum life. She imagined that Harold would pout for a few days, but she decided that would be fine, she'd need some time to ease back into the routine and get over the sadness of letting go of her adventure. Noah would just have to remember her as a plain, old grandma who baked him cakes, rooted for him at his rowing meets and hadn't done one exciting thing her whole life. *Dull, old, responsible Grandma.*

The waitress brought a tray full of food and spread the plates out in front of her.

"Yikes," she said to the waitress, "if I eat all this you'll have to take me out of here on a forklift." She dug in and was halfway through a stack of pancakes and her second egg before she took a breath. The coffee was just the way she liked it—so hot it should come with a warning label and strong enough to put hair on your chest as Harold liked to say.

Merry June realized how starved she was when she finished off a bowl of grits, some hash browns and three slices of bacon. She was finishing her third cup of coffee when she looked outside to see a familiar car pull into the parking lot. She fished around under some discarded napkins and found her glasses to get a better look at the person getting out of the car. It looked like Sally, but this woman's hair was pulled back in a ponytail and she wore a long, loose fitting gray sweater over black tights. The woman slung a large handbag over her shoulder and headed toward the door.

"There you are," Sally said as she slid into the seat opposite Merry June. "Thank goodness I caught up with you."

97

"What are you doing here? I thought you were on your way to Las Vegas."

"I was, I mean I am. And I'm taking you with me."

"What?"

"I was on my way out of town and I put in a Coldplay CD. So, I'm ridin', thinkin' 'bout this and that when the song *Fix You* comes on. You know it?"

"No, sorry."

"Well, anyway, I'm singing along and right away I say out loud, MJ!"

"You said MJ?"

"Right. Don't you get it? It was a sign. I believe in signs, don't you?" She didn't wait for Merry June to answer but went on, her voice animated and happy. "I said to myself, 'Sally, if you don't go right back and get MJ and take her to Vegas with you, I'll never forgive you'." She sat back, out of breath.

Merry June didn't know what to say. On the one hand, she'd come to terms with the reality that this was all a silly plan made in an irrational moment. It was so totally out of character she was surprised her children hadn't sent people after her to lock her up. Here she was— hitching rides and lodging from total strangers. She must really be crazy!

"Say something, MJ," Sally worried when Merry June didn't respond. "You haven't changed your mind, have you? You just can't give up on your dream. You can't do it, you hear me!" She turned agitated and angry; red blotches appeared on her cheeks, and her knuckles whitened as her fingers gripped the edge of the table.

"Sally, I don't know what to say." Merry June thought for a moment. "It seems to me the signs have been telling me all along to 'go home'. Nothing has gone right with my plan from the very beginning. What do you say about those signs?"

"I say those were *tests* to see if you were really serious. I don't think those were signs at all. They were tests," she repeated.

"But this latest thing, losing my ride with Al, being dumped in the middle of the country, for crying out loud. That was just some cosmic test?"

"Right," Sally perked up and helped herself to a forkful of MJ's cold pancakes.

"And now, you're hearing that song, *Fix It*?"

"*Fix You*," Sally corrected.

"*Fix You* or *Fix Me*, that's a sign?"

"Yeth," Sally said with her mouth full of pancake. "You gonna eat that?" she pointed her fork to a piece of bacon jelling beside some hash browns.

Merry June pushed her plate toward Sally, "No, go ahead."

"I don't know what to do now," Merry June said. She glanced across the room at the Western Union desk that would open in another fifteen minutes. She had made her decision and now here she was back on the fence. She looked down at her sensible shoes with insoles "for the mature woman" the saleswoman said right after she'd called her 'sweetie', a word that sent icicles up Merry June's spine.

She thought about the sneakers and then about the toeless pumps she'd worn at the party. She smiled when she pictured them. Harold told her she looked ridiculous, and she surprised them both when she told him to go to hell. He said swearing was very unbecoming in a woman her age and a grandmother to boot. She said she'd earned the right to swear after putting up with him for fifty years and ended with a "fork you" for emphasis. She hadn't quite worked up to saying the actual "f" word yet, but she thought she might.

"Want to see something?" Merry June said, opening her backpack. "This is how I got the nerve to go on this trip." She lifted the pumps from her bag and spread out a napkin before sitting them on the table. The lights from the diner bounced off the rhinestones making them wink and sparkle amidst the debris of the breakfast dishes.

Sally picked one and turned it around in her hands. "These are beautiful," she said. "You wore these to your party?"

Merry June nodded, picking up the other shoe. She told Sally about the fight with Harold and how she'd worn the shoes anyhow. "But what he'd said, those words, ruined how I'd first felt when I bought them. I imagined dancing with my husband, how pretty they were and how they weren't 'old lady' shoes, but shoes for somebody who led a glamorous life." She hesitated and choked back a catch in her throat. "Just for one night, I wanted not to be Merry June Pigg, senior citizen, retiree, housewife, but to be a little special, even impractical and kooky if only for a few hours."

Sally wiped tears from her eyes. "Like Cinderella."

Finally, Merry June spoke. "Sally, I've had a happy life. I don't want to give you the wrong impression. And I love Harold even though sometimes he's such an old fogey that I want to stick his big old bald head in that vice that's clamped onto his workbench and..."

Sally broke out into a laugh that made everyone in

the place turn and laugh with her. "Merry June, is there a 'but' coming up?"

"Sally, I appreciate your offer more than I can say," Merry June picked up the pumps, turned them to watch the rhinestones sparkle before putting them back in her bag, "and..."

The younger woman watched her new friend as she weighed her choices.

"And, I've decided to go with you!"

They both jumped up from their seats and hugged and twirled, laughing and crying all the same time.

"All right, MJ Wedding—let's go be famous!"

THIRTEEN

The women loaded Merry June's backpack into the car and Sally headed for the highway. She turned on the CD player and they listened to Coldplay and Neil Young.

"I like all kinds of music," Sally said. "What's your favorite, MJ?"

"I love James Taylor and The Eagles and of course the Beatles. I was at their concert the time they came to Cincinnati. They were supposed to play at the ballpark but they got rained out so we had to go back the next night. You should have seen that crowd. Boy, did we have fun." Merry June closed her eyes, picturing that night. "I'll never forget it."

"I've never been to a live concert," Sally said matter-of-factly.

"Really? A young girl like you, I would have thought

you went to lots of concerts."

"We never had money for concerts when I was growing up. Too many kids, my dad raising the five of us on his own..."

"Where was your momma?" Merry June interrupted, "If you don't mind my asking."

"She died. She was mowing in the back field and coming up the hill crossing the old bridge above the creek. It had been raining the week before and the creek was high, washing away the bottom section of the hill that supported the bridge. As best as my daddy could tell, the weight of the tractor caused a mudslide taking momma, the tractor, and the entire hill into the creek. The tractor turned over and the roll bar kept the tractor from crushing her, but the water was running high, and she got trapped in her seat belt and drowned."

"That's terrible, Sally. How old were you when that happened?"

"I was the oldest at twelve. My brothers and sisters were two years apart all the way down to my baby brother who was four years old. Naturally, I had to quit school and take care of the kids and the house. Do all the things momma had done."

"But you were still a child yourself."

"Maybe, but I grew up fast. I did what I had to do until my daddy married again. I was fourteen so I hightailed it out of Applecreek and caught a bus out of town. I landed in Raccoon Ridge. Not much of a step up."

As they rode, the women joked, pointed out sights, and listened to music from Sally's large CD collection. They stopped at a rest area where Merry June bought two sodas, bags of pretzels and Butterfinger candy bars from the vending machine. They sat at a picnic table and watched people come and go. An elderly couple walked a little Jack Russell terrier that immediately ran up to Sally and began jumping up her leg.

"Jack likes you," said the woman reining him in.

"Can I pet him?" Sally asked.

"Sure, he loves attention," said Jack's owner.

"Where you girls headed?"

That made Merry June chuckle, as she was clearly as old as this woman. "It's been some time since I've been called a girl," said Merry June.

"Sorry, that just slipped out. My husband, Bob, and I," she said, pointing to a white-haired man leaning against a motor home in the truck parking area, "are on our way to the Grand Canyon. We were there years ago when we took our boys." At the mention of 'boys' her face became serious. She brightened, adding, "We loved it so much we wanted to go back. From there, we'll just go wherever the wind blows us."

Sally spoke up, "That sounds like so much fun. Just ramble around the country, wherever and whenever you please. Someday..."

Sally was interrupted when a truck driver standing in the group talking with Bob called to her.

"Hey, Sal," he said while the others hooted, "Whatcha doin' way over here? Business so bad you had to stake out new territory? Come on over and I'll be your first customer," he yelled while moving his hips suggestively.

"Hey, buddy," Bob said loud enough to cause the others in the group to back away in a circle around the two. He put a hand on the younger man's chest. "That is not cool."

The driver balled up his fists but spit on Bob's shoe instead before he pushed his way through the spectators and started for his rig.

Sally started to raise her hand in the one finger salute when Merry June laid hers on Sally's arm. "Come on, let's go, Sally. You're better than that."

Sally shook off Merry June's arm angrily. "No, MJ, I'm not. This is what I am, a lot lizard, a hooker, that does business out of a shitty old car for truckers and any other man with a few dollars in his pocket." Her voice was hard. "So just deal with it." She walked to her car and called to Merry June over shoulder, "You comin' or not?"

Merry June smiled and waved goodbye to the woman who looked uncertainly at Sally then back at her. She could only imagine what the woman must be thinking but decided she didn't care. Moreover, the fact that she didn't care what some stranger thought, surprised Merry June. That wasn't like her at all.

Back on the highway, the women rode in silence. Once or twice Merry June tried to start a conversation, but Sally just looked stonily at the road ahead and refused to speak to her. The Ford slowed as they entered the foothills surrounding Denver. The Rockies loomed in the distance.

Sally steered the car onto the next exit ramp and into Swifty's Gas and Go. "We need to fuel up," Sally said. "Gimme some cash."

Merry June counted out two twenties from her shrinking roll of bills.

Sally took the cash without comment and went inside to pay. Merry June was at a loss as to what to say or do next. She didn't know why Sally was angry with her. She was hurt and felt like she had made another big mistake when she had taken her up on the offer of a ride.

What is it going to take to convince you that this trip has been a huge disaster Merry June Pigg? She looked at the horizon thinking, *Denver is a big city. If I call Rob to wire some money to me from there, I can catch a flight home.* The idea of her family made Merry June homesick. Right now, all she wanted to do was climb into her own bed next to Harold, wake up to the aroma of fresh coffee brewing in her own sunny kitchen and sit outside on the deck watching the birds at the feeder.

When Sally returned to the car, she pulled an oversized can of Coors beer out of a paper sack that she shoved under her seat. She flipped open the tab and took a long swallow at the same time she turned the key in the ignition.

"You shouldn't be drinking while you're driving," admonished Merry June.

"My car, my rules," Sally said and took another long swallow.

Merry June worried in silence as they got back onto the highway and headed out of town. "Maybe I should just get off here. I think I've overstayed my welcome."

"Yeah, maybe you have."

"Can I ask you a question, Sally?"

"Can I stop you, old woman? That's what you do best." She took another long drink.

"Why are you mad at me?"

Sally didn't answer. She drained the can of beer and tossed it into the back seat.

"You know better than to drink and drive like this. And I don't want to end up a statistic." Merry June was firm.

"Cry me a river, lady," Sally answered. She reached one hand under the seat and pulled out a glass bottle containing clear liquid. Sally squeezed the bottle between her legs, unscrewed the top, and took a long drink. "Wanna swig, MJ?" she said, offering the bottle to Merry June.

"What I want is...Is that vodka?"

"Yeah, Merry June. It's vodka," Sally slurred back. "Don't they sell vodka out in the sticks of Ohio?" She took another long drag on the bottle that was becoming closer to empty with each drink.

"Sally, you're scaring me. Pull over. Now. Please," Merry June begged and her voice broke. "I want to get out."

Sally turned the steering wheel hard onto the

shoulder and jammed her foot on the brake. The old car bumped through the gravel into the weeds. Steam hissed from under the hood until finally, the vehicle let out one long wheeze and shuddered to a stop.

"Well, shit," Sally said as she stumbled out onto the gravel. "Damn you, you worthless heap of crap." She gave the door a vicious kick and still clasping the liquor bottle, staggered along the highway. Merry June watched and waited as the woman paced back and forth in front of the car, swearing and punching the air with her fist until suddenly, her legs folded under her, and she sank to the ground. Merry June leaped from the car and ran to her. She wrapped her arms around Sally's waist in an effort to pull her upright and farther away from the speeding cars.

"Get up this minute," Merry June scolded as though Sally were a disobedient student in one of her classes. "This is ridiculous. You're going to get us both killed. Stop acting like a brat."

Sally looked up at Merry June, astonished that the older woman would dare to speak to her in that way.

"Go away and leave me alone." Sally pumped her legs, throwing dirt on them both.

"Fine. You have your little hissy fit, get yourself run over, but I'm going. Goodbye, Sally. I really did enjoy meeting you but now you're just acting like a two-year-old, so I'm leaving." Merry June opened the back door of the car and retrieved her backpack.

She couldn't resist a few last words. "You've had it tough, Sally. No question. Nevertheless, I wonder just how long you're going to let other people decide your life for you. Get up, get on with it, and take responsibility for yourself. Who's driving the bus? You or those losers back at the rest stop?" With that, Merry June shifted her backpack onto her shoulders and set off down the highway.

FOURTEEN

Merry June couldn't believe she had just told Sally off and was walking along the highway in Kansas or Colorado—she didn't even know what state she was in. *The state of confusion*, she thought wryly. They were miles from Denver, and she was sure she couldn't walk the distance. She considered hitchhiking but decided that given her luck so far, she'd probably be picked up by a serial killer. *Then wouldn't Harold just love to say he told me so?* The idea made her laugh out loud.

She looked back to see Sally still sitting where she'd left her and she looked so alone, Merry June had a twinge of guilt about their fight. She really liked Sally and had looked forward to their traveling together and getting to know her better. It felt like that movie, *Thelma and Louise,* at least until the end when they drove over a cliff.

Merry June drew the line at anything as extreme as that. She did like the part where Thelma—or was it Louise—blew up that oil tanker because the driver made lewd gestures and comments to the girls.

Merry June jumped when a motorhome blew its horn and swerved so close it brushed her jacket.

"Hey." The woman from the last rest stop leaned out the window and waved. The RV pulled up ahead of her and slowed to a stop off the highway.

"What happened? I saw your friend back there. You guys have car trouble?"

Merry June jogged, if she could call it that with her artificial knee, to the RV. Bob stepped out from the driver's seat carrying Jack in one hand and a red leash in the other. He fastened the leash to Jack's collar and walked him down an incline away from the road.

"A disagreement," Merry June said, shrugging. She sighed and shaded her eyes with her hand to look back to where Sally continued to sit.

"That's a shame," the woman said. "She seemed like a nice girl. Very pretty."

"She is nice," Merry June said. "She's just kind of mixed up."

"We have plenty of room if you want to ride with us,"

the woman offered.

"I sure don't like the idea of leaving her here like this," Merry June said, never taking her eyes off the small figure sitting in the dirt beside her beat up car.

"Why don't you get in the RV, and we'll back up to her and you can try to talk to her? By the way, my name is Bonny Rose and I already mentioned my husband is Bob. My friends call me Bonny or Rosie, take your pick."

Merry June introduced herself and Sally and scrambled into the back of the RV with Bonny Rose and Jack. Bob carefully backed up the vehicle to where Sally sat. They all climbed out and formed a half circle around the girl who gripped a nearly empty vodka bottle. She looked up at the threesome, lifted a hand in greeting, and fell backwards, flat on her back.

Merry June knelt beside the unconscious girl and took her head in her lap. "She passed out," she said looking up at Bonny and Bob. Jack licked Sally's face, but she didn't stir.

"She's drunk," said Bob, speaking for the first time.

"What should we do?" Bonny asked Bob.

"Call the highway patrol."

"Oh, no," both women said in unison.

"We'll take her with us," Bonny decided.

"I don't know…" Merry June said, gently smacking Sally's face to wake her.

"It's settled. Right Bob?" Bonny headed for the RV to open the rear door. "Bob, you take her feet and Merry June and I will take her arms."

Even though Sally was slightly built, she was dead weight and getting her into the motorhome was harder than they expected. They gave up trying to pick her up and instead all three grabbed her shoulders and arms and dragged her to the vehicle. Bob got inside and pulled while Merry June and Bonny pushed and lifted and folded Sally's inert body into the cabin. Once inside, they laid her out on the floor and put a blanket over her. Bonny took a pillow off the sofa and scrunched it under Sally's head. Jack jumped up on her stomach and after a full minute of turning round and round, made himself a nest and fell asleep.

"What about her car?" Merry June said.

"Hmm, good question," said Bonny.

Bob scratched his head.

"Can we tow it?" Bonny asked Bob.

"I have a chain. I guess that would work. But we can't take it far," Bob said. He scratched his head and looked doubtful.

"This is really too kind," Merry June said. "You two are on vacation—I can't stand the thought of holding you up."

"Now don't worry, we don't have to be anywhere. That's the beauty of being retired. Right, Bob?"

"Un h huh," Bob said.

"Okey dokey, then, let's get 'er saddled up." Bonny seemed to be having a great time.

Bob went outside and after rummaging around in the rear compartments of the RV, he returned with a chain like something out of a 1950's sci-fi flick. The links were thick and heavy and looked like they could have kept Godzilla secure. He secured one end to a rusty hitch on the RV. He hooked the other end to the underside of the car.

He looked skeptical. "I don't know about this. Car's a junker."

"Now what?" Bonny clapped her hands together and did a little pirouette.

"Now somebody has to get in," he nodded toward the car, "and steer."

"Oh, I will." Bonny swung open the door and hopped in behind the wheel.

Merry June stood watching the preparations with no

116

small amount of trepidation. She reluctantly got back inside the RV, checked on Sally who was snoring along with Jack, and took a seat in the captain's chair next to Bob.

Bob waved his arm out the driver's window to let his wife know he was ready to go then let the RV roll forward slowly under its own steam. He looked back at her and saw her wave happily before he gave the camper a little gas and eased out onto the highway. The little caravan had gone about two hundred feet when a sudden jerk lurched the RV forward. Bonny laid on the horn. When Merry June looked back, she saw Sally's car with Bonny at the wheel sitting in the distance behind the camper. The chain was still securely fastened to the RV— and to Sally's axle that bumped along behind them.

"Bob, stop!" Merry June yelled but he was already pulling off the road. She stepped down from the camper and met Bob at the back. He was trying to haul in the heavy chain, an impossible job since the Ford's axle was still attached. Merry June hurried back to where Bonny sat with her emergency flashers warning oncoming traffic to change lanes.

"Ride 'um cowgirl! Hee haw, what a trip." Bonny leaped out of the car. Merry June pushed her out of the way as far from the road as possible and waited for Bob who came back to help.

No one could believe what happened next. A flatbed truck hauling portable toilets came hurtling over the crest of the hill right at Sally's car. The driver of the flatbed turned the wheel hard to try to avoid a collision, but speed and surprise took their toll causing the flatbed to skid on its side just inches from where the three good Samaritans stood watching while the cab disconnected and plowed into the median. Toilets bounced loose from their tie-downs and splattered their contents on the shoes, hair and everything in between on the shocked trio. Bonny recovered first and yelled at her husband to "Get the camera! Get the camera! My Red Hat ladies aren't going to believe it. This is one for Facebook!"

The truck driver flew out of the cab and across the highway to where the three stood, shocked and dripping.

"Oh, thank God you're all right." Bonny ran over and hugged him in a tight embrace. The foul smelling goo that covered her, now attached itself to the driver.

"Who the hell stopped in the middle of the road," the driver yelled, his face the color of a ripe tomato.

Bob and Merry June stood too stunned to speak. Bonny clapped her hands like she just won the grand prize from the Publishers' Clearinghouse.

"We broke down," she told the driver. "Say," she smiled through the muck dripping down her chin, "any chance you're single? There's a lovely girl..."

...

Bob called 911 on his cell and the driver waved on passersby who slowed down to gawk, take pictures and get a good laugh. Merry June pulled up some grass to wipe her face and whatever it was that was dripping down her neck. Soon sirens could be heard as first the fire department, then the highway patrol and an ambulance all showed up.

"You all want to step over there and get checked out," the officer in charge held his nose and pointed in the direction of the paramedics who hadn't even opened the ambulance doors.

"Stand in a line over there by that hill," one of the paramedics commanded. "Okay, Ricky, let 'er go," he called to a fireman who pointed a fire hose at them.

Ricky turned and gave a thumb's up to his colleague standing beside the truck. That was the last thing Merry June saw before a blast of icy water knocked her off her feet. She felt Bonny sputtering and flailing around on the ground next to her and heard Bob shout "What the hell?"

"I think the correct response is 'what the shit?'" cracked an officer who high fived one of the emergency personnel.

Soon, the tow truck arrived and loaded up the truck and lined up the portable toilets in the medium. Next, a salvage company came and took away Sally's car. Bonny insisted that Bob take her picture in a variety of poses around the toilets until he lost patience and started toward the RV.

"Well, wasn't that somethin'?" Bonny exclaimed.

"Get that shit-eatin' grin off your face," Bob remarked, straight-faced.

The two women collapsed in hysterics.

When they all finally pulled themselves together, Bob said they better wake up Sally and tell her the news about her car. "First, you two wait here a minute," he opened a compartment in the RV and retrieved a garbage bag. "Nobody goes inside. Put you clothes in here—shoes too."

Bonny immediately removed her jeans and t-shirt and put them in the bag. Merry June shook her head when Bonny smiled and said, "You next."

"No way. I don't have anything else to wear except a cocktail dress and high heels. I'll walk from here, thanks."

120

"Don't be silly," Bonny said, "the next exit could be miles away. Bob," she called, "throw Merry June a towel will ya'? She's kind of shy."

Merry June resigned herself to the ordeal and was soon a little dryer and sipping coffee in her anniversary dress. Bonny took the driver's seat and maneuvered the camper back onto the road.

At last, Sally began to stir and when she did, disturbed Jack who greeted her with vigorous kisses and happy sounding barks.

"Have a good nap?" Bob asked Sally.

"What happened," Sally said rubbing her eyes.

"Not too much. Merry June'll fill you in."

FIFTEEN

After Merry June gave Sally the *Cliff's Notes* version of what happened, they pulled into a rest stop where Bonny made everyone iced tea and passed around Little Debby Oatmeal Snack Cakes. They all settled down to decide what to do next.

Sally wept and shook her head in disbelief. Merry June played with her glass, feeling silly in her cocktail dress and sad that her pretty new pumps had to come out only because her sneakers had yuck on them. Bob fidgeted with the map while Bonny flitted around the galley kitchen, refilling glasses of tea and singing *Whenever I Feel Afraid,* from the *King and I.* She was clearly having the time of her life.

Bonny had changed into a cotton duster that was emblazoned with painters' palettes smeared with brightly colored swabs of paint, brushes with fat bristles, jaunty berets and easels. The duster captured the attention of everyone who saw it and made them smile.

"I think this is some sort of sign," she said.

"Please don't say that," Sally said, looking at Merry June with raised eyebrows.

"Oh, honey, but it is. I know signs, and this is a great big one, right from heaven." She lit up like Times Square on New Year's Eve.

Bob grunted. "More like it came from down below," he said and put another snack cake in his mouth.

Sally nodded in agreement.

"Come on you gloomy Guses." Bonny plowed ahead refusing to be discouraged. "We've got plenty of room for everybody. Right, Bob?"

Bob looked up from his map. Crumbs of oatmeal snack cake flew out of his mouth when it fell open. "Huh?"

"Sure, we can sleep six with no problem," Bonny continued. "And I won't take 'no' for an answer." She popped up from her seat, singing *Zip a dee do da* as she got busy pulling sleeping bags and pillows from the overhead compartments.

Sally put her head on the table. "Oh my God."

Merry June asked Bob if she could borrow his cell

phone to call home as hers had died. Wordlessly, he handed her the phone and went outside for a smoke. Sally joined him and the two stood together smoking and exchanging occasional words.

Merry June decided to bite the bullet and call Harold. It had been three days since she'd left and a full day since she contacted Noah who promised to keep the rest of the family updated as long as Merry June promised to text him at least once a day and preferably more.

"Hello?" Harold's deep voice came on the line.

"It's me," Merry June said.

No answer.

"Harold, I know..."

"You don't know anything, Merry June Pigg. If you knew anything, you would know we've all been worried sick about you."

"I don't know why..."

"YOU DON'T KNOW WHY?"

"I've been in touch with Noah every day. Anyway, I just wanted to tell you myself that I'm fine and that I'm in Colorado. It's so pretty here, Harold. I wish you could see it."

"Well, since you've left me high and dry, on my own, to fend for myself, while you go skipping around the whole damn country, not a care in the world, no consideration for your family, I'm soooo glad to hear that 'it's PRETTY' where you are," he snarled and slammed down the phone.

Bob and Sally looked up when Merry June joined them.

"How'd it go?" Sally asked.

"Not so good."

"Want a cigarette?" Sally asked.

Merry June shook her head. "Thanks, but I quit smoking when I was pregnant with Rob." She thought a minute before putting out her hand. "What the heck, I'm having an adventure." This got a tiny smile from Bob who lit the cigarette Sally had provided to her.

"I'm sorry about what happened," Merry June said to Sally.

"That's okay, MJ. I was acting like a jerk. It was just that guy..."

"I know." Merry June hugged her. "He's the loser. Not you, Sally. Definitely not you."

Bob stubbed out his cigarette in the dirt and turned to go with a sigh. "Better go see what Bonny is up to. I've learned a few things living with that woman for the past fifty-two years and that is, it's better to be in on the planning than to hear about it afterwards."

"I can't believe I missed all the excitement," Sally said.

"When those toilets started flying around and the stuff that came out of them..." Merry June shuddered thinking about it. "That image will be burned into my brain for the rest of my life."

"And remember, Bonny has pictures," Bob called back over his shoulder.

"All aboard," Bonny called gaily from the door.

Sally linked her arm through Merry June's and escorted her back to the camper. "It's a sign, MJ, a stinkin' sign."

SIXTEEN

Bob slid behind the wheel and eased the rig onto the highway. The women sat in back and Bonny told them they wanted to make it to Grand Junction by dark where they planned to camp for the night. Unless something else unexpected happened, she told them with a grin, they would be in Grand Canyon National Park by tomorrow evening.

"You mentioned you made this trip with your sons?" Sally asked her.

"Yes, that was a long time ago. Either of you ever been there?" she said, changing the subject.

The women shook their heads.

"How old are your boys?" Merry June probed, feeling there was more to Bonny's story.

"They're gone," she said simply. "Gone. I don't want to

spoil our trip by talking about anything sad. Why don't you tell me how you got here, MJ? And why you have a cocktail dress and those gorgeous shoes." She reached down to run her fingers over the rhinestones. "Would you let me try them on? I've never owned any shoes that beautiful in my whole life."

Merry June slipped off the pumps and handed them to her. "Be my guest." Merry June explained how she'd gotten them for the anniversary party and repeated the story of the fight with Harold over them.

"Men just don't understand," Bonny said, turning her feet this way and that to catch the light dancing off the bows. "I have shoes like this on and I look down and I feel happy all over."

Outside, it was beginning to get dark. Bonny called up to Bob to ask how much longer it was until they got to Grand Junction. He pointed to the highway exit sign indicating they had a mile and a half to go. She asked Merry June if she wanted to look for a Laundromat to wash the clothes she'd been wearing at the time of the accident. Merry June said she wanted to throw them away and find something new, preferably inexpensive.

"Perfect," Bonny said. "We always look for a Wal-Mart when we're traveling."

"To stock up on supplies?" Sally asked.

"Well, that, of course. But it's also where we like to camp."

Sally and Merry June looked at each other.

"You see, some Wal-Marts let folks like us use their parking lot to camp in overnight. It's a good deal for the store because the campers always go in to buy groceries, other supplies, and," she smiled at Merry June, "sometimes clothes. It's great for us too because we save a night's camping fee, and we always meet other RV'ers like ourselves. We trade stories about where we've been and talk about where we're going. We learn a lot about places to see and some to stay away from. We love Wal-Mart."

As she spoke, the familiar blue sign came into view ahead. Bob eased the RV into a parking spot at the end of the row where several other campers had already set up. Merry June and Sally climbed out to stretch their legs while Bonny changed into jeans and a sweatshirt.

Merry June felt silly in her cocktail dress and pumps and told the others she was going into the store to purchase something more comfortable. Sally offered to stay and help get dinner together while Bob took a walk around the makeshift campground to get the latest in tips and gossip.

"You like hot dogs?" Bonny asked Sally.

"Practically raised on 'em," Sally said as she set the table with the paper plates Bonny pointed to in the cupboard.

Bonny opened and shut cupboard doors above their heads that were covered with watercolor pictures of animals, landscapes, city scenes, all done in bright colors and bold brushstrokes.

"Did you paint all of these?" Sally took a step back to admire the collection.

"These are just the tip of the iceberg," Bonny answered. She took one of the pictures down and ran her fingers lightly over the paper. It was the figure of two children sitting on the steps of a red brick house and the only picture where the colors were slightly muted. "Now, I only use vivid, happy colors in my paintings." She fastened the painting of the children back onto the cupboard. "I could paint you, Sally." As she spoke she touched a curl that had escaped from the ponytail. "You have such beautiful red hair and pretty skin. Yes, I will paint you tomorrow. It's all settled."

Sally took the older woman's hand in hers. "I'd like that." Embarrassed, Sally changed the subject. "I could be

130

happy living like this full time, seeing the country. If only I was independently wealthy and didn't need to work for a living."

"Yes, Bob and I are lucky because we've got our Social Security. It's not a lot but it's enough. And being just the two of us..." her voice trailed off and she turned her face away from Sally.

Sally put her arms around Bonny. "I think we're a lot alike. Life has knocked us around, but we keep getting up and hoping for a better day."

"That's beautiful, Sally. You're right." She hugged her new friend back. "I'm so glad we met," she said, wiping away a tear that found its way to the tip of her nose. She brightened and said, "We'll sure have a great story to tell our friends."

The two women worked in silence, each with their own memories. Bob poked his head inside and asked when dinner would be ready and Merry June returned carrying a sack from her shopping trip.

"I was quite the sensation," Merry June said. "This is not your typical Wal-Mart shopper's attire."

Bonny showed Merry June the tiny bathroom where she could shower and change clothes.

"That's better," she said when she rejoined the

others. She was dressed in jeans and a tee shirt with a cowboy riding a bucking bronco and the words, 'Cowboys are better lovers' in sequins across her chest.

The other three took one look and simultaneously broke out laughing.

Merry June smiled with them. "These were on clearance. Only nine dollars for the entire outfit. I got some underwear, socks and pj's too, but those weren't on sale," she added regretfully. "Oh, I almost forgot," she reached into the plastic bag, "I bought us this." She pulled out a bottle of Mogen David wine and proudly set it on the table. "Harold always buys this for us at Christmas."

Her words brought another round of laughter from the others.

"Hot dogs and Mogen David," Sally sputtered, wiping tears from her cheeks. "Oh, MJ, you are hilarious."

Merry June smiled, confused but enjoying the camaraderie all the same.

"I say we have a toast," Bob said, unscrewing the cap and pouring the wine into paper cups. "To new friends," he said, lifting his cup. "May the roads that brought us together, continue to cross."

Everyone chimed in with 'hear, hear' and raised their drinks.

After dinner, Sally and Merry June insisted on cleaning up while their hosts sat outside and relaxed in the lawn chairs Bob had set up. When they'd finished, they re-joined the couple and talked.

"Star bright, star light," Bonny began, reciting the poem they all remembered from childhood.

"What'd you wish for?" Sally asked Bonny, squeezing her hand.

"I wished that we would all stay friends forever."

"Amen," the others said in unison.

SEVENTEEN

Rain pounded against the metal roof of the camper. Merry June peeked out the window from the narrow bed she shared with Sally and saw gray sky and a parking lot dotted with puddles. Sally was already up and gone. *Probably on a Wal-Mart run*, she guessed.

She tiptoed to the bathroom then went into the kitchen to make coffee. Bob and Bonny were still sleeping so she tried to be quiet as not to wake them. She was always the first one up at home. Harold usually slept in until at least nine because he worked late in his workshop, long after Merry June had gone to bed. *Another way Harold and I are out of sync.* When she thought of her husband, she checked her watch. *It's eight o'clock at home. Home*—she felt a twinge of homesickness and wished for a moment that she were back in her own kitchen, drinking her morning coffee and working one of her crossword puzzles.

I think I'll call him she decided and retrieved her cellphone from the charger. *Maybe this time we can actually be civil.*

Harold answered on the third ring, his voice thick with sleep. She thought he sounded alarmed. "What's wrong? You okay?"

"I'm okay," Merry June choked up. "I miss you."

Silence on the other end.

Merry June sighed deeply, "I'm sorry I woke you, Harold. I'm homesick and I thought if I could just hear your voice..."

"You there yet?"

"Not yet. We're still in Grand Junction, Colorado and..."

"We?" his voice rose. "Who the hell are we?"

"Bonny and Bob and Sally. We met..."

"Merry June Pigg don't tell me you're jaunting around the country with total strangers! I thought you were taking the bus. Who are these people? How do you know they're not serial killers on the lookout for old ladies to rob and...," Harold was wide-awake and really yelling now.

Merry June cut him off in a stage whisper, "If they're

going to rob me, they're going to be pretty disappointed." She filled him in on the story of her lost bag, the money and the plane ticket. She finished by telling him how she'd been ready to give up the whole idea when she opened his card and found the five hundred dollars.

"It was a sign, Harold," she told him warming up to the idea of signs. "I bought a bus ticket and well," she sighed, "the rest is kind of complicated."

"I can only imagine."

Merry June, encouraged that he hadn't hung up on her, went on, "Tonight we'll be at the Grand Canyon, then Sally and I will go on to Las Vegas."

"I thought your 'dream'", he spat out the word, "was to go to Hollywood. Be another Betty White or some damn thing."

"Harold, the reason I didn't want to tell you, to ask you, is because I knew you'd be exactly like this; sarcastic, make fun of me, dismiss me, like you did about the shoes."

No answer, just the sound of breathing.

She decided to change the subject. "Are you okay?"

"I'm as well as any man could be whose wife decides to humiliate him in front of all their family and friends, by deserting him—at her own party no less. Other than that,

I'm just fine as frog's hair, Merry June Pigg, if that's still who you are."

"Of course that's who I am." She decided not to tell him about MJ Wedding just yet. "I don't want to fight with you, Harold. I just want to know that you're all right and to tell you," she hesitated, "that I love you, and I miss you, Harold."

Harold's, "Me too," was so muffled, at first Merry June wasn't sure if she heard right.

"I'll call you tomorrow," she said.

"Right," he said, and hung up.

She poured herself some coffee and sat at the table staring into the gray dawn. Lights began coming on in the campers around the lot and she observed men walking around their RVs, checking tires, rolling up the awnings on their rigs and preparing to get back on the road.

A lone van, with a pop-up top sat a distance away from the other campers at the edge of the parking lot. While everyone else had clustered together near the lamppost, the van driver had picked a spot in the shadows. As Merry June watched, the slender figure of a woman opened the passenger door and stumbled out. The woman, now staggering toward their RV, reminded her of someone—*it's Sally. What is she doing?* Merry June gasped out loud when the realization hit her. "Oh no, it can't be true," she said out loud.

The door to the RV opened and the two women stood face to face.

"You're up," Sally observed. Her hair was pulled back in a ponytail but some strands hung around her face. Her mouth, set in a defiant smirk, looked raw and bruised. She smelled of cigarettes and whiskey.

The noise awakened Bonny who joined them in the kitchen. "What happened?" she looked from one to the other.

"Go ahead, tell her, MJ. You know you're dying to," Sally's voice was hard but Merry June also thought she heard fear in it.

Bonny glanced back toward the bathroom when she heard Bob get up. The sound of the shower brought relief to the faces of all three women.

"Let's sit down." Her voice was gentle but allowed for no argument. Merry June and Sally sat across from each other while Bonny filled Styrofoam cups with coffee and handed them around before she joined the other two.

"Okay, let's have it," Bonny looked at Sally expectantly.

"Okay. Since you three totaled my car," she began

defensively, "I have no way to get to Vegas, where," she lied, flipping out her cell phone, "I had, repeat had," she emphasized, "a job lined up waitressing at MGM. Those girls make a couple of grand a week, even on a bad week," she gloated. "But I had to be there by tonight and thanks to you old coots, the chance of a lifetime has gone up in smoke–or should I say down the crapper."

"I see, " Bonny's eyes narrowed, "and since we ruined your chance to parade around in high heels and a leotard twelve hours a day offering free booze and who knows what else to a bunch of conventioneers, you went back to your old job. Did I get it right?"

Merry June watched the fingers of her own hands clench and unclench in her lap. The tension was broken when Bob, who unbeknownst to them had gotten out of the shower and was leaning against the bedroom door, said kindly, "Bonny, let the child explain." He turned his attention to Sally who dropped her face into her hands.

"There wasn't any job," she cried, "I made that up." Her tear-streaked face looked to Bob for help.

Bob nodded, "Thanks for your honesty, Sally. Now tell us what happened."

Sally looked at Bonny. "I can't."

"Yes, you can, honey. I'm sorry," Bonny said and

folded the thin shoulders into her own plump, motherly arms.

Sally took a deep breath. "After you guys went to sleep, I went into Wal-Mart to buy some cigarettes." She peeked over Bonny's arm at Merry June. "I took ten dollars from your backpack, MJ." She cried harder. "I'm so sorry. I'll get my stuff and leave right now," she said but made no move to do so.

"No, you won't," Bonny hugged her tighter. "We'll deal with that later. Now, what happened when you went into the store?"

"I saw this old guy, the one that's driving that old van over there." She nodded at the vehicle Merry June had watched her emerge from earlier. "He came up to me and asked if I was your daughter and well," she waited, trying to figure out how to phrase her next few words, "I told him 'no', I was a nurse aide taking care of you." She looked at Bonny when she said this, "I told him you had Alzenheimers Disease."

Bonny, Merry June and Bob tried to hide smiles.

Sally looked around, "Why? What'd I say?"

Bonny patted her and said 'nothing', she was fine and to continue with her story.

"So, he says, 'what time you get off' and then he starts

laughin' real hard like that was so funny and I haven't heard that line about a million times."

"And?" Bob prodded.

"And I didn't say anything, 'cause I'm considerin' my options, you know? Then, he pulls a hundred dollar bill outta his wallet and says he needs a little nursin' care himself and if I come back to his van and just visit with him for a while, he'll give me the hundred."

Bob balled up his fists and jammed them into his pockets. Bonny squeezed Sally so tight she started to cough. Merry June stroked the girl's hair.

"Go on," said Bob.

Sally began to weep in earnest. Her words sputtered out between sobs.

The story they finally pieced together was shocking to everyone present. Sally agreed to go with the man in the hope of making an easy hundred dollars but knowing all too well that this kind of creep did not give young girls money just for conversation. She convinced herself that she would do as little as she could get away with and still get the money. She told her friends that she tried to convince him to go back in the store to buy some liquor so she could make her escape, but he just laughed and set a bottle of whiskey on the table and after taking a drink right from the bottle he offered her some. Sally said she refused but he grabbed her by the hair and poured what seemed like half the bottle down her throat.

"I never drink when I'm workin'." Sally sat up straight and looked around. "I need to be able to stay on my guard."

Merry June nodded.

"My head hurts," Sally said, "and I think I'm gonna be sick."

"Will you put some ice cubes in that towel?" Bonny asked Bob. She took the towel and pressed it against Sally's forehead. "Can you go on?"

"Do I have to?" Sally pleaded.

"You're doing great," Bob reassured her. "Almost there, and then you can lay down. Okay?"

"He pulled my panties off," she started crying again, "and forced himself into me. He smelled and he was dirty and I was crying because he was drunk, and he wasn't using a condom so he poured more whiskey into my mouth and when I tried to spit it out he held his hand over my mouth. He had black grease or something under his fingernails." She buried her face in Bonny's shoulder.

"Then did he let you go?" Bob asked.

Sally shook her head and laughed mirthlessly, "Not a

chance. He said he wanted his money's worth and kept at it. I was hoping the whole time that he'd pass out or die or anything to get him off me." Her voice got stronger when she told how she'd gotten her knee in between his legs and jerked hard into his groin. "While he was yelling and holdin' himself, curled up on the floor, I emptied his wallet." She turned the thick wad of cash out of her pocket onto the table. "Then I came back here."

For a few minutes no one said a word.

"Where's the cell?" Bonny asked her husband. "I'm going to call the police."

"You can't," Sally cried out. "Please, don't." She was near hysterics.

"We have to, honey. He can't just get away with this."

"You don't get it. I knew what the deal was. I went in there on my own. Plus, I stole his money. If you call the cops, I'm the one who'll go to jail," she pleaded.

Bob counted out the cash. "There's a thousand dollars here." He rubbed his temples. "What Sally said makes sense." He looked at his wife and Merry June who waited for him to go on. "The last thing she needs is to go through another ordeal."

He got up slowly and started for the door.

"Where are you going?" Bonny got up to stop him.

143

Merry June took Sally in her arms now.

"I'm going to have a talk with our neighbor."

The women stood watching from the open door of the RV as Bob marched through drizzle that had turned into a downpour. He pounded on the door of the van and when no one answered, he picked up one of the bricks the owner had placed under his rear tire and hurled it through the windshield. Bonny covered her face and watched from between her fingers.

The door swung open, "What the hell? I'm gonna call the cops," the man screamed. "You crazy old bastard, whadda ya think you're doing?"

Bob could feel the eyes of their fellow travelers on him. He was grateful for the rain that kept everyone inside.

"You sure you want to call the cops?" Bob's strong voice rang out. "I'll dial them right now." Bob held out his cell phone and placed a finger on the keypad.

"That bitch stole my money," the man screamed back.

"Let's talk this over like men," Bob said, the threat in his voice was unmistakable. He pushed the man backwards inside the van, stepped in after him and pulled the door closed.

Bonny held her breath as she watched. Merry June

and Sally clasped her hands and they all waited as the minutes dragged by with no sign of Bob or what was happening inside that van.

"I'm scared," Bonny said finally. "What if he beats Bob up or even worse? He's a lot younger than Bob and he has high blood pressure and..."

The women were all frightened.

"If he doesn't come out in two minutes," Bonny told Sally, "I'm going to have to call the police.

Sally nodded, "I know. It's okay."

They watched and counted the seconds until the door opened and Bob stepped out. His face was grim as he jogged back to the RV.

"Pull one of those sleeping bags down from the overhead compartment, will you MJ? Sally, you heat up that coffee in the microwave. He's soaked through and through."

Bonny met her husband at the door with a clean flannel shirt. She insisted he change out of his wet shoes and socks before he began to tell them what happened inside the van. She brought him his slippers, Merry June wrapped the sleeping bag around his shoulders and Sally set the steaming cup of coffee in front of him. Bob murmured his thanks and sipped the coffee before speaking. He shivered and his wife retrieved an afghan from the couch and tucked it around his legs.

"That's fine," he smiled. He began to settle down and get his shaking under control.

The women fidgeted while they waited for him to speak.

"We just chatted," he began, "and he agreed not to press charges." He turned to Sally and smiled. "And, I convinced him that he owed you the whole thousand dollars all things considered."

"Bob," Sally couldn't believe her ears, "how on earth did you do that?"

Bonny and Merry June joined in peppering him with questions.

Bob held up both hands saying, "Let's just say I have certain superpowers that I only reveal under extreme circumstances. This was one such occasion. That's all I am able to say on the subject."

Sally stared at Bob like he truly had just swept in wearing a blue leotard and a red cape. Bonny and Merry June fussed over him until he was finally able to reassure them that he was fine and that the best way to spend the rainy day was to stay where they were and relax until tomorrow. He gathered the sleeping bag around him and

146

said he was going to lie down for a bit. It was only then that Merry June noticed that his right hand was swollen and bleeding.

EIGHTEEN

When they got up the next morning, the sun was shining and the white van was gone. Bob gingerly touched the gauze wrapped around his right hand from time to time. No one mentioned the events of the previous day. Sally insisted on buying food and other supplies they needed before they set out and nothing anyone could say would discourage her. She returned with a shopping cart full of food and presents for everybody.

Despite their protests and scolding, Sally beamed and insisted they open the presents before they pulled out.

"You first, MJ," she instructed and handed her a fat plastic bag.

"You really shouldn't have," Merry June protested but found herself excited nevertheless. She lifted a soft chenille robe from the sack. "Oooo, Sally, I love it," she said and hugged the girl close.

"Wait," Sally said, "there's slippers too." Like a child at Christmas too pleased with finding the perfect gift, Sally reached in and pulled out fuzzy pink slippers. "Something else," she said and pointed to a small box at the bottom. "Perfume, she announced proudly, "for your audition."

"It's just right, Sally. I'm speechless," Merry June grinned and wept and dabbed perfume behind her ears, then did the same for Bonny and Sally.

"You next, Bob," Sally demanded. The older man's face beamed as he unwrapped a rain poncho, wool socks and a pipe complete with tobacco. "You're already distinguished looking, Bob," said Sally to reassure him, "so right away I decided you should have a pipe."

"You are absolutely right, Sally. I have always wanted a pipe." He turned the gift over lovingly in his good hand. "Thank you, honey."

"And last, but not least, Bonny—for you." Sally handed her a small gift bag and a card.

Merry June could see that a very special bond had sprung up between Bonny and the younger woman. She was happy for them but she to admit she also felt left out and a little jealous.

Bonny opened a card that pictured the Grand Canyon

at dawn with the shadows and light from the rising sun outlining the rocks and cliffs in all their majestic beauty. She read the inscription inside slowly, running her fingers across the handwriting. She carefully returned the card to its envelope and brought a small box out of the gift bag. Opening the box, her face lit up and her eyes misted.

"It's perfect," was all she said. She held the box for Merry June and Bob to see.

Inside was a tiny brush and palette dangling at the end of a delicate gold chain. "I love it. It is perfect."

...

After breakfast and the gift giving, Bonny announced that she would drive since Bob's hand was still sore.

"MJ, I'll need you to spell me," she said to Merry June who turned pale at the idea.

"Me–drive? I don't think I could," Merry June stuttered. "This thing is huge."

"Thirty-six feet long," Bonny boasted.

"At home I drive a Honda Civic. Harold won't let me even touch the steering wheel in the SUV."

"You'll be fine," Bonny reassured her, and the matter was settled. "Now, let's go." She slid behind the wheel and Merry June sat in the passenger's seat so she could 'see

150

how easy it is'. Bob and Sally sat at the table with a deck of cards arguing about what to play. *It feels just like a family vacation*, Merry June thought.

The two women laughed and talked as they traveled. The landscape changed to vistas as far as they could see with rock formations in striated hues of reds and browns towering around them. When the road stretched flat and long in front of them, Bonny eased over to the shoulder to let Merry June drive.

"Just point her straight ahead and you'll be fine," she instructed. "We haven't passed a car for the last hour so this will be a piece of cake. Besides, I thought you wanted an adventure."

When Merry June gained some confidence and picked up their speed to fifty miles an hour, Bonny went in the back to check on Sally and Bob. Sally was asleep on the sofa and Bob in the bedroom. Bonny pulled the cover up under Bob's chin and kissed him on the top of his head. She did the same with Sally who opened her eyes and smiled up at her before falling back to sleep.

...

The sun was dropping below the horizon as the travelers arrived at Trailer Village in the Grand Canyon National Park. Because it was September, there were fewer campers than there would be during the summer months when school was out and park activities were in full swing. As the sun disappeared, so did the warmth it provided. Bonny handed Sally and Merry June sweatshirts and suggested they leave them on to sleep in.

"We might get to see snow on the ground when we wake up." She laughed at the surprise on their faces.

Sally went outside to help Bob set up and together they worked on stabilizing the wheels and setting up lawn chairs around the fire pit the park service provided for campfires. Sally stuck her head inside to tell them she and Bob were going in search of firewood. Bonny and Merry June watched them for a while before turning to their task of preparing the cans of chili Sally had purchased and setting the table for their dinner.

"Looks like Bob has a new friend," Merry June remarked as they sat together talking and sipping glasses of the Mogen David wine.

Bonny nodded, pensive.

"Is there a problem?" Merry June asked.

"No, not at all. In fact, I couldn't be more pleased. She helps him," she hesitated then downed the wine and poured another glass.

"Helps him? You mean with the chores?"

"No, but that's nice too, especially since we're both getting older and things are harder than they used to be."

"How else does she help him?" Merry June prodded.

Bonny swirled the liquid around in her glass. Then she gazed out the window and told Merry June about her boys.

"Donny was ten," she began. "Toddy was eight. Because they were so close in age, they were almost like twins. They were best friends. Did everything together. Hardly ever fought like a lot of brothers." She stopped and went into the bedroom and brought back a photo. It was of two boys in matching striped tee shirts. The older boy, Merry June guessed since he was a lot bigger than his brother, wore a Cincinnati Reds baseball cap and held a baseball. His younger brother held a baseball glove on his lap and grinned into the camera. His two front teeth were missing.

Bonny stared at the picture, patting the faces with her fingers.

"Toddy was small for his age and he took a lot of teasing from the other boys. Donny was getting into a lot of fights protecting Toddy and it seemed like Bob and I were at the school every day over a new incident. Then one day, Toddy came home real excited. He'd been invited to join a club some of the boys in his class started. They built a clubhouse down by the creek at the end of the street and they told Toddy he had to keep it a secret—especially from his brother." Bonny passed a bowl of pretzels to Merry June.

"The boys told Toddy before he could be a full-fledged member, he'd have to be initiated. Toddy didn't care, he was just so eager to belong, he agreed." Bonny dabbed her eyes. "Donny wasn't far off. He was playing baseball and he could hear the shouts of the boys, including Toddy, playing in the woods. One of the kids Donny was playing with told us afterwards that a bunch of kids came running out of the woods calling for help. Toddy had fallen in the creek that was higher than normal from recent rains."

Merry June put her hand over her mouth.

"You've guessed what happened next. Donny went in after Toddy but by the time help came, both of my boys were gone."

NINETEEN

The next day, the foursome toured the park. The vast beauty of the canyon awed Sally and Merry June. Bob and Bonny loved showing off the spots they visited before and exploring new ones. That evening as they sat around the campfire watching Sally make S'mores, Bob cleared his throat, "Bonny and I have been talking," he said, "and we have something we'd like to talk to you both about."

Bonny nodded at him, so he went on. "We'd like to invite you both to travel with us for a while, spend some time here," he spread his hands, "in this magnificent place. Then, we can take you to Las Vegas."

Sally clapped her hands and jumped up and hugged them each in turn. "Thank you. I'm in." She turned to Merry June and pulled her to her feet, dancing her around the fire. "What do you say MJ? Sound great? Will you come?"

Merry June felt Bob and Bonny watching her, and she knew they already knew what her answer was going to be. She hugged Sally and kissed her on the cheek. "Honey, I'm so happy for you but I have to get back to Harold and to my family. I'm not sure I can make it to California even if I want to. I'm almost out of money and I've already been gone too long. I've been thinking about my situation all day and I realize it's time for me to go home. Getting this far, meeting Rufus, Al, you three has been an amazing gift. I feel that I've been hunting the wrong fortune—that it's been right in front of me all along." She took Sally and Bonny's hands and squeezed them hard.

Sally poked the fire and they watched in silence as the sparks flew upward and disappeared in the chilly air.

"Anyway, I think it's a sign," she paused and said, "Lord knows I've had an adventure."

They sat and watched the fire die and the stars crowd the sky like an endless stream of diamonds tumbling over a black velvet carpet. Few words were spoken as each one sat alone with their thoughts and mused about what the future might or might not bring. It felt as though there were only tomorrows ahead and the past had finally been put to sleep. All except for Merry June. She felt the shadow of everyone and everything she loved casting a spell over her and despite her little speech, she had no idea where she was going.

...

The next morning, Bonny, Bob and Sally drove Merry June to Flagstaff where she intended to call Harold and talk things over with him. She stood alone in front of the bus station and waved her new friends out of sight. She shifted her backpack and smiled as she pictured Bonny finding the pumps she'd left in her closet. She hoped she'd get to dance in them someday soon.

She found a seat in the corner of the small station and dialed home. When she got the machine, she decided not to leave a message but to call again later. Next, she left a text message for Noah telling him where she was and asking him to have Harold call her. Merry June counted out her visibly shrunken roll of bills. She had less than two hundred dollars left and she still had five hundred miles to go to L.A. She was told the cost to Los Angeles was seventy-six dollars, which wouldn't leave enough for even a cheap hotel room once she got there.

When Harold called an hour later, Merry June gave him the abbreviated version of the past two days. "So I'm in Flagstaff, at the bus station," she said.

Harold ignored that and instead talked about the weather, told her he'd seen Conny and Ed every day and they always asked about her. "Of course, I had to tell them no one has heard anything from you for the past two days. That you were traveling with some gypsies who probably murdered you and threw your body in the desert for the vultures to eat up. "

"Oh, for cryin' out loud, Harold. You have to stop watching those TV crime shows. Your imagination is getting away from you."

"*My* imagination? You really think you can get on *Fortune Hunt*? You're out of your mind. Besides, I need you here. I'm running out of frozen dinners and Conny had to do a load of laundry for me. You are my wife, Merry June Pigg, not some silly movie star," he snorted.

"Harold?" she tapped the phone against the wooden bench. "Harold? Sorry, you're breaking up," she lied. "I'll have to call you later." She hung up.

Merry June sat and thought; after her conversation with Harold, her pride wouldn't let her admit to him that she'd failed and she wanted to come home. She reassessed her situation, counted her money once more and realized if she spent the money for bus fare, she'd have to sleep on the street once she got there. Her cell chimed just then with an incoming text from Noah checking to see if she'd heard from Harold. She texted back saying she had and told him about her money trouble. He responded by asking if he should ask his dad to wire money and after thinking it over, she told him 'no', she wanted to do this on her own even if it meant turning around and going home. After all she'd made it this far.

She decided to check out the neighborhood for someplace to have coffee while she thought about what to do. A sign ahead flashed 'Eats' so she went inside. Except for Merry June and the lone waitress, the place was empty.

"Just coffee, please," she said.

"Big surprise," the waitress said. "Cream?"

"Yes, please. And where is your restroom?"

Merry June couldn't remember the last time she'd washed up properly but when she took one look at the stained sink and empty soap dispenser, she changed her mind. "I'm building character—and immunities," she said under her breath.

The waitress came back with a beat-up metal coffee pot, a stained ceramic mug and a handful of powdered creamers. She returned to a TV perched on the end of the counter where a soap opera played out a daily grind of misery.

Bonny and Bob had insisted she take some granola bars, beef jerky and trail mix, 'just in case'. Merry June tried to act inconspicuous as she reached into her backpack for a handful of trail mix.

A teenage boy came in and sat in a booth facing Merry June. He had greasy blonde hair and wore a sweatshirt with some words that Merry June couldn't make out and jeans that barely clung to his skinny hips. He stared at Merry June and without taking his order, the waitress brought him a large soda that he sipped while he watched her.

"Hi," she said, forcing a smile. She tried to appear friendly so he wouldn't see she was afraid.

"'Sup?" he snarled, his face hard.

"Not much. 'Sup with you?"

"You makin' fun a' me old woman?"

"No, I'm definitely not doing that," Merry June looked outside praying somebody, hopefully a police officer, would come in right about now.

"Then mind yo' own damn business." He sucked noisily on the straw.

Merry June pretended to be fascinated by the cars

driving past their window when she heard a rustle coming from where the boy sat. She refused to look up until she felt rather then saw, the boy slip into her booth. When she finally found the courage to raise her eyes, he was leaning across the table leering.

"You ain't from the neighborhood," he said.

Merry June instinctively gripped her backpack. "No."

"Where'd ya get that shirt? Pretty racy for an old broad."

Merry June folded her backpack across the cowboy on her chest.

He grinned wider. "So why don't you show me whatcha got in that bag?" His hand slid across the table; he waggled his fingers for her to hand it over to him.

Merry June shook her head, clasping the bag tighter.

An ad for Depends, something Merry June wished she were wearing, came on the TV. The waitress looked around at them, shrugged, and resumed her watch.

"You must have a bag full of money there. What's yer name?"

"MJ." She was trembling all over.

"MJ?" he said, disbelieving. "What kinda name is that? You ain't lying to me are you, MJ?"

"No," was all she could manage.

"No? Well then MJ, let me take a look in that bag. I mean for all I know you might have somethin' dangerous in there. Maybe a gun? Maybe you came to rob ole Zelda over there." He pointed with his head towards the waitress who didn't turn around but must have been listening to their conversation because she held up her middle finger at this last remark.

"No, I don't have a gun," her voice shook with the rest of her body.

"I don't believe you, MJ. You look like a dangerous criminal to me," he said, deadpan. "I might have to come over and take that bag right outta your skinny old hands. Is that what you want, MJ?" He started to rise from his seat.

When Merry June saw what he meant to do, she reached for the coffee pot and swung it against the side of his head with all her might. She heard bone crack and saw blood stream from a gash on his cheek. She clasped her bag, made a dash for the door and stumbled out onto the street. She ran as hard as her artificial joint would let her until she reached the crosswalk where she stopped to wait for the light.

Merry June looked back to see her would-be attacker standing in front of the diner, one hand up to his head.

Blood covered the side of his face as he screamed obscenities and called for somebody to "Stop that old bitch." The few pedestrians around walked past without even a glance at either of them.

The light changed and Merry June looked back once more to make sure he wasn't coming after her, then turned and walked as fast as her seventy-year-old legs would let her until she reached the bus station.

TWENTY

It took Merry June fifteen minutes to stop shaking and slow her breathing to normal. She couldn't believe what just happened. She was shocked at how she'd reacted, but she knew there was no way she was going to allow some punk to put an end to the dream she'd already sacrificed so much for. *If anybody is going to do that, it will be me.*

"I need chocolate." She looked around for the vending machines. "I think this calls for a lot of chocolate." She took a five out of her wallet and bought five packs of Reece's Peanut Butter Cups. "Better." She opened the third package, licking chocolate off her fingers and not minding the germs or the stares.

"I'm proud of you MJ. You've changed." She realized she was talking out loud when the man sitting next to her slid to the end of the bench, blocking her from his sight with his newspaper.

She didn't care. She felt strong and empowered. A voice in her head told her she could do anything she put her mind to, and she visualized a thumb's up for bravery.

"I may be brave, but I'm still stranded," she said to the voice in her head. She realized this wasn't the kind of neighborhood where she wanted to test her fighting skills a second time, so she decided to stay in the bus station and figure out what to do next.

A middle-aged woman, her blonde curls swinging and her deep blue eyes outlined in black, pushed through the door. She wore tight fitting, cobalt blue slacks that flared above white leather boots. Her white blouse shimmered with sequins and set off her flawless complexion. Merry June couldn't help but stare; *she must be a celebrity or an actress. I wonder what she's doing in a crummy bus station?*

The woman checked the bus timetables posted on the wall and spoke with the teller at the ticket window. A distinguished man with dark, curly hair shot through with silver joined her.

The woman approached Merry June. "Excuse me, but I wonder if you've seen a girl, she's eighteen, with long brown hair down to here?" She held her hand waist high. "She was scheduled to arrive on the bus from

Albuquerque an hour ago. We were supposed to meet her but we got hung up in traffic."

Merry June thought a minute and said she had been there when the bus arrived, but she didn't notice any girls that fit the woman's description.

"Thanks anyway. Sorry to bother you."

"No bother at all. I've got nothing but time," Merry June sighed.

The woman turned around. "Is everything okay?"

"Yes, no, I mean, I'm not sure right at this moment." Merry June was tired. The sugar high had dissipated and the adrenaline rush of the earlier confrontation bottomed out. She could barely keep her eyes focused on the woman who sat down beside her.

"Are you okay? You don't look too well." The woman asked.

"Thanks, I'll be fine. I had a busy day and just now feeling the aftershock, I guess."

"What's your name? Is there somebody we can call for you?"

"I'm MJ. MJ Wedding." The name was beginning to sound natural, as though it belonged to her, the actor.

"What a pretty name. I'm Charlene, Charlene Shepard, and that's my husband, James, over there. My sons are next door at the video arcade. Teenagers," she shrugged. "We're supposed to be meeting my daughter, Peggy here. I can't imagine what's happened to her."

"Did you try her cell?" Merry June's motherly instincts kicked in.

"Yes. No answer."

"How about texting her?"

"I hadn't thought of that. I'm not sure I know how."

"Here, we'll do it on my phone. I've gotten pretty good at it since that's about the only way I can communicate with my grandson, Noah," she added.

Charlene sat with Merry June to wait for news from her daughter. Immediately a text message came in saying she'd missed the bus and would catch up with them in Las Vegas.

"That girl was three weeks late being born and she's been late ever since," Peggy's mother said.

"I know what that's like." Merry June thought of Noah and smiled. Her phone chimed again. "Wait a minute, here's another message. She says she's got a big surprise."

"If she makes it to the show on time, that will be a surprise," Charlene shrugged. "Come with me, MJ," she held out her hand, "and let me treat you to lunch. Then you can meet the whole family."

Merry June blushed recalling her brush with crime. For all she knew the police were looking for her right now. She decided she better keep out of sight as best she could. "I can't but thanks for the invitation."

...

It's do or die time, MJ Wedding. Heads it's do and forge ahead to see this trip to the end or tails it's die, the adventure stops here. She took a quarter out of her pocket and tossed it in the air. She held her breath and watched the coin spin on the tile next to her shoe. She squeezed her eyes shut and counted, "one, two, three." She stared at the coin lying on its side—heads.

Merry June checked the schedule and found the bus to Vegas didn't leave until eight o'clock the next morning. She purchased her ticket, paid two dollars for a bottle of water from the vending machine and using her backpack as a pillow, lay down on the bench to close her eyes and rest. When she woke up, six pairs of eyes were staring down at her.

"What time is it?" Merry June rubbed her eyes and checked to make sure her backpack was still there.

"You've been asleep since I left, I guess," Charlene checked her watch. "That was nearly two hours ago. It's after three now."

"Thanks for waking me," Merry June said, "I'm surprised I haven't been arrested for," she stopped before telling this seemingly decent family about her recent crime spree. "For vagrancy," she said.

Charlene's husband offered his hand. "James," he said, "James Shepard. You already know Charlene. This is the rest of my flock. Our sons, Mark and Luke and my sisters, Jane and Dawn." He gestured to the others who waved at her.

"We were talking about you," James said. Charlene's curls bounced up and down. "And we wondered if we could offer to drop you someplace?"

"We're concerned that you're hanging out in a place like this by yourself," Charlene chimed in. "It's not a real good neighborhood and you seem like somebody," she struggled for the right words, "somebody who might be a target for something bad," she finished, flustered.

Harold would certainly agree, Merry June thought and after the incident at the diner, both he and the Shepards might have good cause to question her sanity. "I'm fine," she lied. "My bus doesn't leave until tomorrow morning so I'm just going to camp out right here. Save the price of a hotel, you know. I'm kinda on a budget," she added, understating her situation by a mile.

"Where are you headed?" James asked.

"Los Angeles, by way of Vegas," she added. "I'm waiting for the bus to Vegas," she liked saying 'Vegas' instead of Las Vegas. It sounded cooler.

"We're headed there ourselves," James said.

"And we've got the room, especially since Peggy won't be traveling with us," Charlene said.

"I don't know. There's so many of you," she immediately realized her slip. "Oh, I'm sorry, what I meant was..."

"It's okay." One of the boys who stood listening to all this came to her rescue. "There are a lot of us, but," he said, "we really do have enough room. See that bus out there," he pointed. "That's ours. We're a gospel group. We call ourselves *The Good Shepards*," he added with pride. "Ever hear of us?"

"No, I haven't," said Merry June, "but that's amazing."

As if on cue, the whole family broke into *Amazing Grace*.

"What do you say, MJ? Can we add another lamb to our flock?" asked James.

"I once was lost but now am found," sang Merry June, gathering up her bag.

TWENTY-ONE

James explained that Arvel Montag, who played the fiddle and sang bass, was the other member of the group and would meet up with them in Las Vegas. He went on to add that Arvel was re-joining the group after an incident following one of their performances in Vegas. He told her Arvel had been shot in the rear end when he tried to marry a woman and her husband got wind of it. Arvel's story was that he had no idea she was married and since he'd only met his bride-to-be less than six hours before their intended wedding, he said there just hadn't been a lot of time to find out everything there was to know about her.

"He had to lie flat on his stomach for six weeks while his wound healed," Jane added.

"But," James said...

"You said butt," Mark screamed and poked Luke in

the side. The boys thought this was hilarious.

"As I was trying to say," James smiled indulgently at his sons, "Arvel is meeting us at Circus Circus where we're scheduled to perform. We like doing shows there since there's a campground right behind the casino that makes it really convenient."

...

Merry June had never seen anything like the Shepard's bus; leather sofas, marble countertops, with stainless steel appliances in the kitchen that gleamed and sparkled. "Wow. My friends Bonny and Bob would sure love to see this. I thought their RV was nice but this is..."

"Amazing?" James said and smiled.

Merry June smiled back as she ran her hand along the buttery leather of the captain's seats where the driver and the passenger could enjoy a panoramic view through the wraparound windshield.

Luke helped her stow her bag and they all took their seats for the short trip. Mark pointed out the old Route 66 historic marker and Luke identified various plants and varieties of cactus along the road. As they got closer to the city, casinos sprang from the desert sand, each seeming a mile long, stretching, blinking, and beckoning with promises of instant riches.

M$. FORTUNE

Charlene pulled the RV under the grand arches of Circus Circus and found a space at the rear of the building where simple pop-up vans camped beside gleaming motor homes some even larger and fancier than the Shepards'. James went inside to check in with the hotel and locate the show manager while the boys, having seen it all before, nagged their mother to let them go inside to the video arcade. Charlene gave them permission, laying down the rules and telling them to meet back at the suite in an hour to go over their homework before the show.

"Homework?" asked Merry June.

"We follow a home school program that allows them to keep up with their grade level. They might want to do something besides sing when they grow up and James and I want to make sure they have a good education. We want them to be able to follow their own dreams and not have to follow ours."

Merry June told the women about her dream and how following that dream had allowed her to see so much more of the world than she'd ever imagined. She told them about all the wonderful people she'd met, and some of the not so wonderful, like the horrible man in Grand Junction and the boy back in Flagstaff.

Charlene said, "My pastor once told me that 'they say

173

it takes all kinds but I'm not so sure we need them all.'"

They all agreed there was a lot of wisdom in that saying.

When James returned, he surprised Merry June with a key to her own room.

"I couldn't," she said. "I am grateful for the ride, but..."

"Courtesy of Circus Circus," James told her. "All part of the fringe benefits that goes with being a performer."

"Don't you stay in the bus—in the back?"

"Sometimes James and I stay in the bus," said Charlene. "We get tired of hotels and this feels like home."

James handed keys to Dawn and Jane who liked to share a room. He and Charlene would take the suite with the two boys. A key was left at the desk for Peggy to pick up when she arrived. Arvel had already checked in and would meet up with them later.

"We'll call you around eight, MJ, and we can all have dinner together before the show," James said.

...

Merry June gasped when she opened the door to her room. She was on the thirty-eighth floor, higher than she'd ever been in a hotel before. The drapes had been pulled back allowing a panoramic view of the city that took Merry June's breath away.

174

"It's like a scene from *Ocean's Eleven* with Frank Sinatra. I'll pretend I'm Angie Dickinson," she told the young bellman who gave her a blank stare.

She walked around the living room that was larger than hers back home. She was awestruck by the bathroom and immediately drew a bath filling the tub with bubbles that perfumed the air with a light, flowery scent. Candles lined the rim of the tub and Merry June lit them all. A flat screen TV was mounted on the wall so she sank into the warm water, turned on the television and watched an old black and white western starring Alan Ladd.

When the water chilled down and her fingers puckered up, she reluctantly got out of the bath. She was putting on the white terry cloth robe and slippers provided by the hotel when she heard a knock at the door. She thought it must be one of the Shepards and opened the door to a woman dressed in the hotel uniform.

The woman smiled and pressed the handle of a shopping bag from the gift shop into her hands. "For you," the woman said in broken English

"There must be a mistake. I didn't buy anything."

"From Senora Shepard," the woman explained. "Have

175

a nice day, Mama."

Merry June brought the package inside and dumped the contents onto the couch. Heart embossed tissue paper hid a pair of soft, black wool slacks and a cashmere sweater in the palest of pink. But that wasn't all. Black shoes of supple leather, a matching Coach handbag and a creamy silk scarf completed the ensemble. Merry June smiled when she saw that Charlene had included several pairs of lacy panties and bras.

She immediately went to phone Charlene to thank her. "It's all so beautiful," she told her. "I can't begin to thank you."

"Seeing you all dressed up for your first night in Vegas will be thanks enough," Charlene told her. "And it's for putting us in touch with Peggy, don't forget."

Merry June laid the items carefully over the back of the sofa before easing down into a recliner and swiveled around so she could watch the city light up in the dusk of the evening.

She wavered on whether to call Harold. She didn't want to chance an argument with her husband right now and spoil this incredible experience. The setting was so beautiful, the images of the clothes fresh and soft, the generosity of the Shepards and thoughts of the other amazing people she'd met, warmed her from head to toe. Instead, she texted Noah a brief message to tell him where she was and that she was fine. She would be in L.A. by tomorrow night and promised to contact him again when she arrived. She added a footnote asking him to pass on the message to Harold.

TWENTY-TWO

Rested, bathed and wearing her new clothes, Merry June felt like a new woman when she met the Shepards in the hotel lobby. She was so profuse in expressing her thanks to Charlene and to the whole family for all they had done for her, Jane begged her to stop.

"I'm starving," Luke tugged at his mother's hand.

"Me too." Mark hopped from one foot to the other.

"Ready to do the Vegas conga?" Dawn asked her.

"Sorry?"

"The buffet line," she explained. "You'll never go hungry in this town. Ready?"

The family, and Merry June, escorted by the boys on either side, headed for the buffet. Merry June said the only buffet Harold ever took her to was Golden Corral unless it was a wedding reception that in their circle of friends typically consisted of cold cuts with sides of baked beans and potato salad.

"We were in Cincinnati once, remember, Charlene?" James put down his fork.

She nodded. "We had that Cincinnati style chili everyone told us we had to try."

Merry June's eyes lit up. "We love it," she enthused. "I always get a five way—the works; chili with beans, onions and cheese piled on a big plate of spaghetti," she added when Dawn looked puzzled. "What did you guys think?"

Charlene and James smiled at one another.

"Interesting," James said diplomatically, making Merry June laugh.

"I guess it's an acquired taste."

They finished dinner and James told Merry June they had to get ready for the show. Charlene was worried because Peggy hadn't shown up yet and she asked Merry June to send her another text message. Merry June followed the Shepards to the theatre where they were to perform two shows later that night. The auditorium was small by Las Vegas standards, but Jane assured her they always played to a full house.

"You can watch from the wings," Charlene told her. "Meanwhile, would you like to wait with me? That way,

I'll know when you hear from Peggy."

The family split up into their respective dressing rooms. Merry June followed Charlene and watched her change into a blue sequined gown and silver high heels that matched the fringe on her dress. She tied up her hair and pulled on a blonde wig with silver ribbons woven into the long waves. Merry June told her that now she looked like the angel that she really was.

Merry June's cell rang indicating an incoming text. "Oh, sorry," she told Charlene who looked around expectantly, "it's from Noah. He's letting me know he got my earlier text."

Merry June could tell Charlene was worried about her daughter and wished the girl would either show up or call. She scrolled through her inbox and was double-checking her voice mail when the door swung open and the missing Peggy burst in. A flurry of embraces and introductions followed when a man who had been watching the scene from the doorway, coughed and raised his eyebrows at Peggy.

"Momma," said the girl, "I have some news."

Charlene looked at the young man standing close to her daughter.

"Momma, this is Randall, and," she went on hurriedly,

"we're married."

A person could have heard a pin drop in the silence that followed that announcement. Charlene fell backwards onto the couch, her hand over her mouth, and stared at the couple. Randall didn't say a word but had the good sense to step behind his wife in case her mother decided to throw something.

"Charlene," Merry June stepped in, "I'm going to find James. I'll be right back." At least Randall knew enough to look nervous when he saw Merry June go out of the room to search for his new father-in-law.

Merry June followed the sounds of a fiddle down the hall and knocked on the door. A man who resembled a grizzly bear answered. Merry June introduced herself to Arvel as a friend of the family and briefly filled him in on this latest development. Arvel grinned and with fiddle in hand he led the way to James's dressing room. "This ain't good," Arvel said. "Best let me break it to 'im."

James smiled quizzically at Arvel who stood in front of Merry June. "Hey man," Arvel said, "Peggy's here—with her new husband."

James opened his mouth to speak—right before he fainted.

TWENTY-THREE

When James came to, he called a family meeting in Charlene's dressing room. There wasn't much room but they all squeezed in together; the boys sat on the floor, Charlene and her daughter huddled miserably on the couch and Randall stood next to James who had a strong grip on his new son-in-law's arm. Merry June tried to leave saying this was a private matter. James took a vote and it was unanimously decided that she should stay. James said Randall's 'no' vote didn't count since he wasn't 'officially' a member of the family.

Peggy alternately wept and glared at her father. Randall shrank into himself, as he stood surrounded by Shepards. The phrase 'like a lamb to slaughter' came to Merry June's mind. She covered her mouth with her hand to hide a smile.

"Tell us," James said, looking sternly at his daughter,

"where and when you and," he fought for words, "this person, met."

Peggy wavered between dread and stubborn pride as she told her family how she met Randall when the family was performing in Lexington, Kentucky. He was at the show with his parents and as she put it, they fell head over heels in love right then and there. Her father tightened his grip on Randall's arm. The young man's face turned the color of a boiled cranberry that was ready to pop.

Peggy wiggled away from her mother and stood next to her husband, her arm protectively around his waist. "That night, he came backstage and from then on we started texting and seeing each other whenever we could."

"How could you see each other?" her mother asked. "We're on the road most of the time and if Randall lives in Kentucky...?"

"Randall's job has him traveling a lot too," Peggy said with pride. "He delivers magazines to grocery stores in the Midwest region. He's on the road, I'm on the road and well, we'd make sure we'd be on the same road as often as possible, didn't we honey?" She had to stand on tiptoe to kiss his cheek. James squeezed Randall's arm even harder until Peggy intercepted, "You're hurting him, Daddy. Stop it."

"A magazine salesman," James groaned. "It's even worse than I imagined.

Arvel, who had been standing unnoticed in the corner, let out a hearty laugh. "Sorry, man. Couldn't help it." When he couldn't get his laughing under control he left the room.

"What do his parents think of all this?" James addressed his question to his daughter. He ignored Randall who tried to speak.

"We haven't told them yet," Peggy said defiantly. "We're leaving tonight to go to Lexington and tell them."

"Tonight? You mean after the show?" Jane spoke for the first time.

"No. I'm sorry everybody, but I can't do the show. My place is with my husband." She stuck out her chin.

At that, they all began talking at once; protesting, arguing, and telling Peggy she was out of her mind. The commotion continued for several minutes while the newlyweds stood silent, arms around one another's waists, facing the first of those tests that all young couples, and older ones too, must endure if they are to survive.

Randall finally spoke over the confusion and succeeded in quieting the room. "I know this is a shock and we're sorry we had to tell you like this." He smiled down at the upturned face of his young bride. "I could only get two days off work and by the time I got here, and we got married and all..."

"Hold it right there, young man," James stopped him. "Do you mean you JUST got married? Here, in Las Vegas?" He couldn't believe what he was hearing while at the same time he thought he saw a possible way out of this catastrophe.

"Yeah," Randall said warily, looking at Peggy who turned pale.

"Well, then," James shouted jubilantly, "we'll have the marriage annulled. It hasn't been consummated!"

Peggy paled even more. Randall smiled and shook his head. James looked from one to the other, "You don't mean...?"

His daughter nodded.

James covered his face with his hands. He knew when he was beaten. Charlene rose, hugged her daughter, and told Randall he'd better take care of her "Or else." She wiped her eyes then announced that the family had a show to do. "So, 'let's get crackin'."

"Call us," were Charlene's final words as she picked up her guitar and smoothed her hair.

When the newlyweds were gone with hugs and kisses for Peggy and a chilly handshake for Randall, James turned his attention to the problem at hand, that of finding a last-minute replacement for Peggy. His sights landed on Merry June.

"Hmm," said Charlene, catching her husband's eye. "I think I have something that'll work." She disappeared into a rack of glittering dresses and boas and surfaced with an armful of ice colored sequins and feathers. "Put this on," she commanded Merry June who watched, confused and not yet aware of what they were asking of her.

"What? Why? I don't know..." Then it dawned on her. "Oh, no. I couldn't," she protested. "I'm not a singer or..."

"You said you wanted an adventure, MJ Wedding," Charlene's voice was calm. "Well, this is an adventure. And besides, we're counting on you to help us out of a jam. That's what friends do." She looked meaningfully at Merry June.

"But I can't sing," she protested, "and I certainly can't play any instrument. Except the piano and that's been a long time."

"Not to worry." Charlene pulled Merry June's sweater over her head, buttoned her into a sequined blouse and wrapped a silver tipped white boa around her neck as she talked. "You can hold the tambourine and just shake it once in a while, whenever the spirit moves you."

"Well, I wanted to make my mark in show business," Merry June said. "My friends," she said, thinking of Sally, Rose and Bob, "would say this is a sign. I guess it is." She smiled at the friendly faces around the room.

A man poked his head in the room, held up two fingers and said, "On in two."

"Ready?" Charlene smiled, "You just stay right near me. It'll be fun."

They filed onto the stage singing, *Put Your Hand In The Hand* to an enthusiastic crowd. They performed nonstop for the next hour and a half to a standing room only audience that clapped and sang the familiar gospel tunes along with them. After the first song, Merry June relaxed and finding she too knew most of the songs, whispered the words right along with the others, and occasionally remembered to shake her tambourine.

"Good show everybody," James said. Jane and Dawn congratulated Merry June and kidded her about becoming a regular member of the group. They repeated the performance again at midnight to the second standing ovation of the night.

"Now are you ready to go have some fun, MJ?" Arvel asked after they had all changed back into their 'civies' as Luke said.

"You mean that wasn't fun?" Merry June said.

"Honey, that was work, my day job," he chuckled. "You ever been to Vegas before?"

"No," Merry June admitted. "I've never been farther than Indiana before."

"Then, MJ Wedding, you stick with Arvel and I'm gonna show you a little slice of Vegas."

"Hold onto your wallet, MJ," Jane warned.

"She's not kidding," Dawn chimed in. "I let him talk me into a night on the town once, and I'm still trying to make up for it." She jingled a handful of quarters.

"You mean gamble?" Merry June looked at the Shepards who were finding all of this very amusing.

"It's not gambling if you stick with ole Arvel," the big man grinned.

"Don't let him pull that on you, MJ," Dawn said. "But, you really should see some of Vegas. There's no other place like it."

"You're welcome to stay another night," James said.

"I appreciate your generosity," she was interrupted by protests from the whole family, "but I have to get to California. I didn't expect to be gone such a long time and..."

"And then, there's Harold," the Shepards sang in unison.

Arvel rose from his seat and held out his hand. "Come on, MJ, let's go and do the town." He winked as Mark, Luke and Charlene pushed her out of her seat.

"Aren't you all coming?" she asked the family.

There was a collective groan from the group and protests of 'too tired, are you kidding, do you know what time it is, and been there-done that.'

"Bunch of party poopers," Arvel said.

"Have fun, kids," James waved. "Just have her home by curfew, Arv."

...

When Merry June woke up and looked at the time, it was four o'clock. "It can't be," she said aloud. "It's daylight. Have I been asleep all day? I can't believe it."

She had never slept an entire day away in her whole life. But then, she'd never stayed up all night partying either. When Arvel showed her the famous 'Strip', Merry June was awestruck. She had never seen so many people;

crowding the streets in the middle of the night, filling the casinos, and throwing wads of cash around like so many beads at Mardi Gras.

She looked around the hotel room. *It looks like it's been ransacked*. Her new clothes lay in a heap on the floor, a wadded ball of cash sat on the nightstand, and an empty bottle of Maker's Mark lay on its side on the dresser. It was all beginning to come back to her. She tried to sit up, but the room started to spin, her stomach churned, and her head felt bigger than a balloon figure at the Macy's Day Parade. She sank back into the covers and held on to the sides of the bed waiting for death.

She thought she heard a door open and then she saw Arvel, standing at the foot of the bed. He smiled broadly and held up two Starbucks coffees, "Venti," he said. He sat on the edge of the bed. "Mornin' Sunshine, or should I say 'afternoon'?"

"Oh, nooo. What happened last night?" she moaned and pulled the sheet over her head.

"Welcome to Las Vegas, MJ." A bigger grin spread across his grizzled face. "Once you found out the whiskey sours were free, you started swilling those suckers like mother's milk. You can really put away your liquor, MJ," he added with a hearty laugh.

190

"I think whatever I put away is coming back out." She grabbed her mouth and made a dash for the bathroom.

"Feel better?" Arvel asked when she tottered back to bed. He poured her a glass of water and added some melting ice from the bucket. "First drink this. Most important thing to remember when you have a hangover," he said, ignoring her glare, "is to rehydrate. Water is nature's cure for whatever ails you, MJ."

She drank the water and swallowed the aspirins he handed her. She pointed to the coffee, and they sat together sipping the rich, life restoring liquid.

"Wanna hear the good news?"

She started to nod but was stopped by the sledgehammer that swung into her forehead.

"You won some money."

"Use it to buy a gun and shoot me."

He waited.

"How much money?" she opened one eye and looked at him.

"Two thousand dollars."

"What?" The sound of her own voice was like a nail through her skull.

"Yep. Does that help ease the pain?"

"No. Well, a little." She was starting to think she might

live but still wasn't sure that she wanted to. "How?"

"Roulette. It's your game, MJ."

"I don't even know how to play roulette." She was getting grumpy which Arvel saw as a good sign.

"No, you sure don't." He shook his head.

Merry June held her finger up to her lips. "Shhh."

"Sorry," he whispered. "Beginner's luck for sure. You were laying down on anything and damned if you didn't keep winning. You were up ten grand at one..."

"Ten grand?" she screamed. The sound of her own voice pierced her skull like an ice pick. She gripped her temples with both hands.

"Ten thousand dollars!" she whispered. "I won ten thousand dollars?"

"Yeah, but then your streak started to turn." He looked miserable. "You started losing but you wouldn't leave so," he wondered how much to tell her before he plunged in, "so I had to pick you up and carry you out of the place. I brought you back here—with your remaining two grand."

She was embarrassed to ask but figured she had lost that right so she asked, "My clothes? The whiskey?"

"You carried on so about me dragging you outta the casino, you said at the very least I owed you a nightcap. I bought the bottle off a guy on the street." He laughed when he saw her stricken face. "Don't worry," he said, "It was empty when I got it. I paid a bum twenty dollars for an empty bottle of booze." He shook his head in disbelief. "We got up here, you passed out, I helped you undress and put you to bed. I slept on the couch." He twisted his neck making a popping sound. "And that's it."

TWENTY-FOUR

The next morning, Merry June squeezed her new clothes into her backpack and said goodbye to the Shepards. Despite her protests, Charlene insisted on paying her two hundred and fifty dollars for her performance and with that added to her gambling windfall, even minus the cost of a bus ticket to Los Angles, she was able to breathe easier for the first time since she began her journey.

...

The bus made its first stop outside the city at the airport. The driver told Merry June this would be her best choice for a reasonably priced motel and was accessible to Culver City by metro. He helped her down from the bus and wished her luck with *Fortune Hunt*. "I'll be watching for you," he called before he shut the door and drove off.

"See, Harold," she said out loud, "most people are really nice and they don't all live in Ohio." She looked to see if anyone was in earshot. "I hope I'm not turning into a funny old lady that talks to herself." She pictured the woman at the bus station in Cincinnati.

She spotted a sign in the distance above a red brick one-story structure that advertised as an Extended-Stay, Eco-Lodge for thirty-nine dollars a night, plus tax. *It looks nice and the price is right. And it's within walking distance so I can save cab fare.* Her spirits lifted by the minute.

When she registered, she was shocked to see fees and taxes added to the thirty-nine dollars, increased the cost to a whopping seventy-two dollars a night. "Holey moley," she said as she counted out three hundred and sixty dollars for five nights. "I may not have to stay that long," she told the pimply young man behind the counter. "I'll be entitled to a refund if I..."

The youth shrugged and pointed to a sign behind him that read 'No Refunds' in large black letters.

She put her change in her fanny pack, retrieved her belongings and headed through the small lobby.

"Gonna need sheets and towels?" the clerk called after her.

Merry June turned around, not sure she heard right. "What?"

"Sheets and towels? Ten bucks a night extra. Eco—

ecological—get it?"

"Oh, I thought it meant economy," she stammered.

The clerk snickered. "Right. Welcome to California."

She paid for two sets of linens and checked out the modest furnishings in the narrow room: the clock and TV that were bolted to the wall, a worn bedspread, and the grimy window overlooking an empty parking lot. She rolled up the bedspread and put it in the corner of the room and made up the bed. Next she went to the front desk for directions to the city bus stop that would take her to Sony studios.

Once she had the maps and information she needed, she was prepared to call Harold and let him know she had arrived safely. She decided to tell him as little as possible about Las Vegas, the boy in the diner or the Shepards. Time enough for all of that when she got back home. *It's always easier to apologize rather than ask permission* she thought.

"Harold, is that you?"

The voice that answered the phone was fuzzy.

"Yeth."

"What's wrong?"

"Cold."

"You're cold?"

"No, I HAVE a cold, Merry June. Like you'd care," he added with a loud sniff.

"I'm sorry, Harold." Guilt swept over her but she brushed it off. Harold was a grown man. He'd get over a cold. *Unless*, she thought, *it was something worse. Pneumonia, an insidious lung disease? What have I done? Killed my husband*?'

Get a grip, she told herself. *Don't be such a drama queen.* She felt her spirits lift.

"Your suitkath is here."

"My suitkath?"

"Thas's what I thed."

Relief flooded over her. *Another sign.* "There's an envelope in it and my plane ticket. I need you to deposit the cash then buy a money order. I'll give you the address of the motel where I'm staying so you can overnight mail that and my plane ticket to me."

"But I'm thick."

Merry June suppressed a giggle. *You got that right.* She took a deep breath, "Harold, I need you to do this for me."

No answer.

"Harold?"

"Otay."

Harold was worse than a small child when he got sick. Merry June was a little glad she was several thousand miles away.

"Thank you, Harold."

They talked some more, mostly about how Harold had gone through all the frozen dinners Merry June had prepared, worn all the new underwear and had to resort to actually cooking and doing some of his own laundry. She didn't even ask him how he'd gone through so much food and clothing in the short time she'd been gone. She didn't want to think about what condition the house was in; she imagined dirty dishes piled in the sink and dust so thick on the furniture that she could write her name in it. She sighed, figured she at least owed him a sympathetic ear, and when she saw that she was down to the last bar on her cell, promised to call him the next day after her visit to the studio.

She felt a huge burden had been lifted knowing that her suitcase was with Harold and her plane ticket, cash and credit card would be arriving tomorrow. She decided to take the bus to Culver City and treat herself to a nice meal. She also decided it would be a good idea to find out where the studio was located so she could arrive early and at least assure herself a seat in the audience. She had missed her audition date but she hadn't come all this way for nothing. And, she would go to the producer, explain what happened and beg to be rescheduled.

The bus driver pointed out the Studios when he dropped her off. She wrote down the intersection and double-checked the bus schedule for the return trip. She'd chatted with the driver on the mostly empty bus and learned the best bet for an inexpensive lunch was a family operated diner off the main drag. He warned her it was kind of hard to find but gave her directions and told her that if she got lost, anybody could point her in the right direction.

Merry June found the restaurant after just a couple of wrong turns. She was famished and realized she hadn't eaten all day.

"A chili burger, fries and a chocolate malt," she told the server.

He took the menu and smiled, "Hope you're hungry. That's a lot of food."

"I'm starved. I have been traveling for days. From Ohio," she explained.

"Really? Where? I graduated from Miami in Oxford."

"I can't believe it. I'm from Shandon. My kids went to Miami too."

"I'm Ryan." He extended his hand. "Nice to meet a fellow Midwesterner. What are you doing out here?"

Merry June told Ryan about turning seventy and giving herself this trip as a birthday present.

He told her he'd get her food and asked if he could join her. "It would sure be nice to talk to somebody from back home."

"Me too. Don't get me wrong. I've met some wonderful people on this trip. Really nice folks, at least most of them." She didn't like thinking about the man in the van or the boy from the diner. "But people from the Midwest are just different—I can't put my finger on it."

"Down to earth," Ryan said. "Solid, family values."

She told him how she'd gotten an audition for *Fortune Hunt* but because of all the problems she had getting here, she'd missed it. "But I'm determined to at least get a chance to be in the audience," she said with determination. "I didn't come all this way to be turned away at the door."

"Say, what are you doing tomorrow? I might be able to help you out. Meet me here tomorrow morning at eight. It's my day off and I'm going to help you get to see," he held his hand out with a flourish, "ta da,".

"Just like Willow," she said and clapped her hands.

200

"My friends would say this is another sign. Thank you, Ryan. I'll be here."

The manager was giving Ryan 'the look' so he shook Merry June's hand and headed toward the kitchen. "Goin' to hunt my fortune," he sang as he disappeared.

TWENTY-FIVE

Merry June was too excited to sleep much. She woke up early and showered and took special care with her hair. She shook out the slacks and pink sweater that were the gift from Charlene Shepard, slipped on the leather pumps and transferred her belongings to the Coach bag. She played with the ivory-colored scarf and put it into her bag. She'd ask Ryan his opinion about it.

The motel didn't offer breakfast so Merry June walked across the parking lot to McDonald's. She nursed a senior coffee and egg burrito for about an hour then left for the bus stop. The sun was coming up and it looked like they were in store for another beautiful day. Merry June loved the flowers that grew everywhere. It was the one thing about southern California that she wished she had at home.

She arrived early in Culver City so she found a bench

to wait for Ryan. Rush hour was like rush hour in Cincinnati and everywhere else she guessed. She thought about what Ryan had said about Mid-western values and decided he might have been wrong and so had she. Thinking of Rufus, Al, Sally, Bonny, Bob and the Shepards, Merry June decided that good people came from all over.

"Hey, MJ," Ryan said coming up behind her. "Ready?"

"I sure am," she turned and smiled.

"Then let's go." He took her hand and walked so fast, Merry June had to trot to keep up with him.

When they hurried past the entrance to Sony studios, Merry June got worried. She pulled back. "Wait a minute. Why aren't we going in?"

"I've got a surprise for you, MJ, but we have to hurry. We have to get there a little early."

Merry June stopped walking. She should have asked this before, but she'd been so excited about the prospect of getting to see her favorite game show in person, she guessed she'd just put it out of her mind. "Tell me what's going on, Ryan. Can you get me into the show or not?"

Ryan's demeanor was different today; the planes of his face were hard, his mouth was a thin, red slash. He huffed in exasperation and checked the time with his cellphone. "Trust me, MJ. Do you want to stand here, possibly miss the chance of a lifetime, forget everything you've been through to get here while we stand around and argue?"

Merry June's gut instinct was to turn around and go back to the studio on her own. She would just be honest, explain why she missed the scheduled audition, and throw herself on the mercy of whoever was in charge. Even in Hollywood, people had feelings and mothers and grandmothers. They'd understand. All those thoughts ran through Merry June's head—and she ignored them.

"Here we are," Ryan stopped in front of the entrance to the City Hotel. Merry June hesitated and peered inside to the darkened lobby.

"Come on," Ryan urged, gripping her elbow and propelling her through the entranceway. "Quit stalling. You're wasting my time," he said, his voice harsh.

"My buddies are upstairs," he said in answer to her raised eyebrows. "This way." He gave a thumb's up to a man behind the desk who returned the signal and smiled, a toothless grin.

He led her through a shabby lobby dotted with dusty potted palms and a sleeping figure stretched out on an antique-looking sofa that was stained and frayed. "Almost there."

"I've changed my mind," Merry June said stopping before a metal door when Ryan reached for the knob. "You're up to something and I'm going to leave now."

"Oh, no you don't, MJ," Ryan said. He shoved her through the doorway.

Merry June looked up the flight of steps and saw a mass of black curls. A second head of hair joined the first, followed by a bare arm sporting a tattoo of a heart with a ribbon twining through it. She thought the only thing left was to have the word 'Mother' on it.

"Hey, man," heart tattoo called to Ryan.

"Hey, Little Ray."

"This is our canary?" Tattoo extended a hand to pull Merry June up the stairs and inside the open door. She turned to face a wall of computers, blinking and scrolling through rows and columns of numbers, code and what else Merry June couldn't even imagine.

"I'm Little Ray and this is Mac," tattoo introduced her to the other man.

"Hi guys," Ryan shook each man's hand. "What's shakin'?"

"Same ole," said Mac. "This here's MJ?"

"So, you wanna be on TV, MJ?" Little Ray asked. His face was close to hers and his breath against her cheeks was hot and foul-smelling.

"I guess so, I mean yes," said Merry June stepping back. She wondered how on earth she was going to get out of here. "Do you work for the show?" She looked from Mac to Ray.

Mac grinned at her then at Ryan. "Let's just say we have access to certain information. Information on potential contestants, the questions for each show, auditions data."

"Wait a minute. Are you hackers?" Merry June was really worried now.

"Hacker is such an ugly word, MJ. We collect data. We're more like researchers." Little Ray laughed.

"That's nice," Merry June thought hard, "but I don't want to be on anymore. I want to go home. My husband's sick and..."

"Now MJ," Mac wheedled, "You're here now, you've seen our er, operation. So, I'm sorry, but you're going to be a contestant. We're sure of it." Ryan joined in the laughter with Mac and Little Ray.

"I don't understand," Merry June was confused. "Why do you three care? What's in it for you?"

"Why, MJ, we just like to troll for old ladies and make them famous. Just think of us as talent scouts." More laughter.

"Ok, MJ," Ryan led her to a seat in the center of the room, "all you have to do is go to the audition, try out, and get on the show. After you win, you can go back to College Corner or whatever podunk town in the sticks you come from and watch the grass or corn grow or whatever the hell people do there."

"Ryan, do you mean you never really went to Miami or even lived in Ohio?'

"No, that's all true. The operative word is *from*, MJ. Life with the hicks in the sticks isn't for me. California is where the money is and I'm following the money, MJ. Following the money."

"But I probably won't win. Then what? Just let me leave and I won't say a word to anyone. I promise. Besides," she was pleading now, "I don't know anything. I wouldn't even know what to say. I have no idea what you're doing. Really."

"Oh, you will win," Mac said. "And you'll get to be on television. But don't you worry your old gray head, sweetie, 'because we'll take care of your prize money. We wouldn't want any ill-gotten gains to be on your conscience." The three men high-fived each other and laughed.

"And guess what, MJ? You have a real good shot at that bag of gold. One hundred thousand Gs. Now isn't that worth hanging around for?" Little Ray pinched her cheek.

Ryan explained further, "You're our canary, old woman. You're gonna help us test our system and then you go home—home to your husband, your dull little life, your garden club and your cat. And we're gonna keep findin' game show wannabes to help us get rich. Ever hear of the quiz shows, *Twenty-One* or *The $64,000 Question* from the fifties?"

She nodded and swallowed hard. "They were fixed. There were huge scandals."

"Glad to know you're old brain is still workin'. And now it's you who's gonna help make us rich, MJ," Ryan said. "Only today," his voice was harsh, "we have some high-tech help." He pointed his chin at the wall of computers.

"What if I refuse? What if I go to the police?"

"You really don't want to do that," Little Ray leaned in close. "You see our operation is very mobile. We'll be on the move the minute you cash our check."

Mac blew her kiss. "Bye, bye birdie."

"And keep in mind, MJ, now you're part of the scam so running to the police will only land you in jail," Ryan sneered. "Meanwhile, we'll be on our way to the next 'opportunity'."

"Okay, listen up," Little Ray said, "Ryan here is going to tell you exactly what you'll do. He cupped her chin in his hand. "You be a good little old lady, MJ."

TWENTY-SIX

Ryan followed Merry June down the hall to a service elevator. They rode to the twenty-fourth floor and exited into a large ballroom where at least a hundred people stood in groups, whispering and watching the closed doors at the end of the room. Ryan gripped Merry June's elbow and steered her toward the table marked 'Registration'. A dark-haired woman in a fawn-colored silk blouse sat behind the table and smiled up at Ryan. Her nametag read 'Tara'.

"This is MJ Wedding," Ryan told Tara. "And she wants to be a contestant."

Tara handed Merry June a folder of forms to fill out and bring back to her.

"Okay if I help my *mom*?" Ryan asked Tara.

"Of course," Tara smiled back and winked.

Ryan took the forms from Merry June and replaced

them with forms he slipped out of his jacket pocket, already filled out. Together, they returned to Tara who gave Merry June a nametag and told her to have a seat and wait with the other contestants.

Tara smiled at Merry June. "I have a feeling you'll do well, MJ. Here are the rules for the audition that you'll need to study. Don't slip up," she warned.

"Yeah, don't mess this up for us," Ryan menaced.

Merry June didn't know what their plan was, but she knew she had to figure out a way to get away. She stared at the so-called set of 'rules' Tara had given her. It was really a list of questions. Merry June guessed these would be used in the audition. And—they had given her the answers!

Her face registered the shock she felt and when she looked up at Ryan, he nodded, "You got it MJ."

When it was time for the auditions to begin, Tara called in the hopeful contestants in groups of twenty-five. Merry June saw that according to her nametag, she was in the last group. That was fine with her as it gave her time to figure out a plan. She sized up the number of security officers in the room and counted only two, one at each door. Tara's staff numbered eight that Merry June could see although she thought there were probably more inside. The other unknown was how many others were in on the scheme. It dawned on her that she could be implicated as part of the scam. Proving herself innocent might not be easy.

"Don't think about that," she said under her breath.

"What'd you say?" Ryan watched her warily.

"Just trying to remember all this," she wiggled the cheat sheet. "You probably should have picked a younger shill," she said sarcastically. "A younger brain that could retain stuff better."

"True," Ryan said. "But you were the patsy who walked into my gin joint," he leered.

It was finally Merry June's turn for her tryout. She started to walk into the audition room, when Ryan stopped her. "Put this in your ear," he handed her what looked like a high-tech hearing aid. The slim wire fit into her ear and was invisible to anyone who didn't know it was there.

"This microphone transmits every sound in the room back to Little Ray and Mac. Every question and answer is recorded onto one of the computers you saw earlier. If you get stuck or forget one of the 'clues' we gave you, Mac will tell you the correct answer." Ryan patted her cheek, "You can't lose, *mom*. And," he gripped her elbow so hard she let out a yelp, "don't try anything funny. Think about the canaries, MJ—the ones who didn't get out alive."

...

Merry June was herded into a room with a set resembling the one Merry June watched on television every night. There was even a woman dressed in a floor length, green evening dress, accented by gold, high-heeled pumps who welcomed the players and reviewed a few rules regarding the audition. "During this session, we are looking for enthusiasm, likability and a positive screen presence. When our producer taps you on the shoulder it means you have been eliminated and we will escort you from the room to pick up your 'thank you' gift.

Merry June, caught up in the moment briefly forgot her predicament and joined the other candidates who jumped, and cheered and clapped. Out of the corner of her eye, she saw Tara tap several people on the shoulder and escort them quickly from the room. The remaining hopefuls cheered and clapped even harder in an effort not to be eliminated.

Next, candidates were chosen at random to join the hostess at the board and play a quick round. The woman in the evening gown stifled a yawn as she flipped squares revealing questions. Contestants who didn't answer fast enough fell victim to the dreaded 'tap' until finally it was Merry June's turn to play. As she was hustled up to the front, she tried to determine if the hostess was in on the scam or not. She couldn't get a read on the bland, bored-looking young woman.

Mac's voice crackled in her ear, "Don't get clever, MJ. Think about those poor dead canaries."

The man next to her took his turn at the board and the game was on. It was Merry June's turn. The category *Opera* was uncovered.

"Not my best category," she stalled. "I don't ..." She searched the faces around her, desperate for a way out.

"Easy, old woman." Mac read the answer into her ear. Merry June took a quick look around the room and parroted the answer from the earphone.

The answer was no sooner out of her mouth than a wall of large men in black suits sprang seemingly from nowhere and surrounded Merry June. One of the hulks pulled handcuffs from beneath his coat and whipped her hands behind her and snapped the cuffs shut. The contestants stared openmouthed, lights flashed, and an applause soundtrack blared in the background while the hostess made a beeline for the exit. Out of the corner of her eye, Merry June saw Tara inching her way toward the door when a fat security guard rushed to intercept her getaway and tackled her to the ground.

Mac screamed epithets in her ear. Merry June struggled against her captor until she managed to break free, duck past the suits and head for the doors. The last thing she remembered was a second guard yelling at her to stop and when she kept moving, he reached in his belt.

"Gotcha, granny." A giant jolt of electricity knocked her to the ground.

The would-be contestants moved to the perimeter of the room to watch the spectacle unfold while the guards assessed the situation. Merry June lay on the floor, rigid, throwing around cuss words like a sailor just denied shore leave. The suits tried to regain control of a situation that was fast unraveling and called for backup from hotel security. It looked as though the other contestants were on the verge of a riot as calls to 'tase the old bat again' turned into a chant from the crowd that was turning into a mob as they watched their dreams of fame and fortune disappear.

And it was all Merry June's fault.

TWENTY-SEVEN

Merry June was stunned. Seated in the hotel's security office, her back was killing her where she had been tasered and she was angry and scared. Ryan and Tara sat next to her then were joined by Mac and Little Ray. All four shot her looks that could intimidate a pit bull.

Officers from the Culver City Police Department crowded into the room with the studio security guards and the three black suits. Merry June's bad knee was becoming more and more painful causing her to squirm in her chair in a futile attempt to find a more comfortable position.

"Stop wiggling around, lady," one of the suits said.

"I'm sorry, officer, but it's my knee." Tears sprang to Merry June's eyes.

"It's Agent," the giant said, ignoring her complaint.

"Agent Clueso," he snarled and flashed a badge under Merry June's nose.

"Wow," said Merry June, forgetting her pain. "You're with the FBI?"

"Or are you the Pink Panther?" Ryan joked.

"Gee wise-guy," Agent Clueso shot back as he stepped forward to crush Ryan's foot under his own massive one, "I've never heard that one." He smirked at Ryan who let out a howl of pain. "Got any more jokes, boy?" he said, drawing out the word and mashing Ryan's foot like he was killing a cockroach that refused to die.

"No sir," Ryan croaked. He stared at the pulp that used to be his foot.

"Alright then." Clueso pulled back and turned his attention to Merry June. "When did you join this bunch of mommas boys—and girl?" He grinned at the foursome. "You the new brains of the outfit? We didn't know about you, MJ Wedding Pigg." That brought guffaws from the entire room.

"The brains? You really think...?" Merry June sputtered. Her knee hurt from the fall, her back was killing her from the taser and now she was being accused of trying to cheat on the television show she loved. It was just too much. She answered by bursting into tears.

The officers looked at each other uncomfortably. They looked unsure about what to do with her. Ryan, Mac, Little Ray and Tara had already asked for lawyers. Merry June insisted she had done nothing wrong and was herself a victim. She also thought about Harold's reaction to the expense of hiring a lawyer even if it meant keeping her out of jail. *He'd probably think I deserve to be in jail for being so naïve on top of everything else. Hopefully, he'll never find out about this little incident,* she thought. She started adding up all the events of the past week that she'd have to mentally lock away in her 'never tell Harold' File.

"I think I need to see a doctor about my knee," she told the men after she pulled herself together. One of the police officers nodded and put in a call on his radio.

"While we're all just chatting," said Agent Clueso, "Any one of you care to tell me how your little gang of misfits here planned to pull this off?"

Merry June raised her hand.

Clueso sighed, "Yes?"

"I'm not really part of this gang. I was kidnapped on my way to the audition. You see, I lost my plane ticket and had to catch a bus then I missed the bus in Grand..."

One of the other black suits held up his hand, "Stop,

lady. We already know the story of your cross-country adventures. Agents are talking with some of your so-called friends as we speak."

"What? Surely you don't believe any of those wonderful people are connected in some way to this," she fought for the word, "this bunch of crooks," she ended lamely. Tears returned as she pictured Al or Rose and Bob, The Shepards or Sally being dragged into police stations and grilled like criminals. "Please, Agent," she begged, "Don't get them involved in this mess. I could never forgive myself."

He thought for a moment then said, "Were you on the lam from some other job?"

"What?" Merry June was both a little flattered and a lot astounded that anyone could believe that she was a hardened criminal. "No, sir, you can't really think, I mean, that I," she stammered, "I haven't even had a speeding ticket since I was twenty-two and that was only because I was hurrying home because I realized I'd left the roast in the oven and it had taken me longer than I thought at the BMV. Unless you want to count the time I got arrested for shoplifting but that was all a simple misunderstanding. I just put a box of condoms in my pocket because Harold was too embarrassed to take them through the checkout himself. That was before the pill, you see and…"

"Enough already! Jeez, lady." The suit was red-faced with frustration. "Save it for the judge."

"Judge? You mean you're going to arrest me? Oh, I can't be arrested again. My husband, his name is Harold, he'll just kill me."

"I'd let him off if he did," said the fat security guard. The others, including the four co-conspirators, all nodded in agreement.

"If you'll just return my cell phone," Merry June pleaded, "I can text my grandson and he'll tell you I'm not a criminal. I'd rather you spoke with Noah because Harold, Rob and Allison—they're my kids, except," she remembered, "for Harold, he's …"

"Your husband," everyone in the room said in unison.

Merry June was saved from further explanation by a knock at the door.

"You call for an ambulance?" A woman in a uniform with 'Culver City EMT printed on her pocket, stuck her head in the room.

"Oh, my goodness," said Merry June, "Thank you, Miss, but I don't need an ambulance. I just need a doctor to look at my left knee. See, I had it replaced last year and when that man," she pointed to the fat guard, "tackled me, I think I bruised it or something. But see," she stood up and tried to do a squat, "I can still do this."

"You need to come down to the hospital and get checked out before we can lock you up," said the officer in charge. "We don't want to be accused of mistreating our perps."

The female EMT waved for her partner to come in and between the two of them, they wrestled Merry June onto the stretcher and buckled her in. At this, terror overrode Merry June's show of nerve and she burst into tears again.

"Please don't throw me in prison," she wept and grabbed the fat guard's hand. "I'll never make it in the 'big house'. I'm just a little old lady..."

"Get her out of here. Now," the officer in charge shouted to the EMTs. "And keep her!"

The lawyer for Ryan, Mac, Tara and Little Ray arrived. She met briefly with her clients and admonished them not to say a word. Each one was handcuffed and led outside, followed by Merry June who was handcuffed to the gurney. A phalanx of reporters and photographers shouted questions at the caravan. A camera flash left Merry June blinded momentarily and the next thing she knew she was being loaded into the back of an ambulance.

The FBI, the police, and the hotel security guards left together and decided they needed to re-convene in the downstairs lobby bar.

"That's one tough old lady," Agent Clueso observed.

TWENTY-EIGHT

Merry June waited in a cubicle in the emergency room of the Culver City Hospital. A policewoman was assigned to stand outside the door. *Do they really think I would try to escape even if I wanted to?* She wondered how anyone thought she could get away handcuffed to the bedrail.

A nurse pulled back the curtain and held it for a small Asian woman who strode up to Merry June. "I'm Dr. Nygen," she introduced herself. "I understand you had an accident this morning and you think you may have injured your knee?"

Dr. Nygen listened to Merry June's story and ordered an x-ray. Waiting for the results, Merry June thought about what she'd done. She still couldn't believe she'd been arrested and was on her way to jail. She wanted more than anything to be at home, listening to the whirr of Harold's tools coming upstairs through the vent as he worked on some new project. There was no way she was going to even try to explain this to him or Rob and Allison. She wasn't even sure how Noah would deal with this latest development.

I can just hear him now," Merry June said out loud, "'Gramma, you got some 'splainin' to do'." She smiled picturing her grandson's face. "At least no one back home will hear about it."

"Everything okay?" a nurse looked in.

Merry June nodded. "Just a crazy old lady talking to herself."

The doctor returned and told Merry June her knee looked fine and that she probably just bruised it in the fall.

"Not a fall," Merry June said firmly, "A take down. I was tasered."

"I heard," Dr. Nygen said wryly.

"What's going to happen to me now?"

"I'll make a medical report to the police and I'm going to recommend that we keep you here overnight for observation."

"Thank you, Doctor." Merry June was grateful for the respite.

"I'm going to order something to help you sleep. Is

there anything else I can do for you before I go?"

"No, I'll be fine, Doctor. You've been so kind. Thank you."

"Goodbye, Merry June. And good luck."

Merry June had never felt so alone in her life even though patients, doctors, nurses and other hospital staff working in the busy ER surrounded her. The guard outside her door checked in on her wordlessly and a nurse brought her some pills that sent her into a kind of twilight sleep.

She drifted in and out of sleep until an aide brought her coffee and a breakfast of bacon, eggs and toast. She wasn't the least bit hungry, but she forced herself to eat anyway. *Who knows what I'll get in prison.*

A nurse came in to take her blood pressure and as she left, she instructed the guard to unlock the handcuffs 'so the prisoner can get dressed'. Merry June asked if she could have her purse back so she could call her family.

"Sorry, Miss. You'll have to wait until you're processed before you can make your call. The squad car's outside now so we need to get going for your court appearance."

The nurse helped her to stand and although she felt shaky and a little lightheaded, she was able to take a few steps unassisted.

"I'm sorry, Miss," the guard said, "I'll need to put these back on you," he held out the handcuffs.

Merry June put her hands behind her so he could fasten the cuffs. He held onto her arm as he walked her through the hallway to the waiting car. Merry June kept her head down avoiding the stares of the people in the waiting room. *I guess this is what they call the 'perp walk'.*

Once in the back of the police car, Merry June tried to make conversation with the officers driving her downtown. They ignored her except for giving her long looks in the rearview mirror. The cruiser pulled into a parking lot at the rear of the station and the officers walked her inside. She was fingerprinted, photographed and patted down before a policewoman took her to a windowless room with a single metal chair.

"Make yourself comfortable Miss Pigg. An officer will be with you—eventually."

"Would you mind bringing me a magazine then? *The Atlantic* or *The New Yorker*, preferably. Also, I would love a coffee—cream and sugar please. And I need to wash my hands."

"Sure, your highness," the officer said, "and how about a nice massage or a pedicure too?" She slammed the door shut and Merry June could hear laughter coming from the hallway.

...

The room was completely empty of furniture except for the chair where Merry June sat. They'd taken her watch and her shoes during intake and not only were her feet getting cold, but she had no idea how long she'd been sitting there or what time it was. She was so tired, she dozed off until her chin smacked her chest and woke her up.

After what seemed like hours, the policewoman who had laughed at her earlier opened the door and motioned for Merry June to follow her down the hall. They walked past rooms marked 'Interview 3, 2 and 1 before reaching the large receiving area Merry June remembered from her processing.

The officer led her to the window where a policeman sat behind a barred window. He shoved her backpack and a large manila envelope through the opening. "Check to make sure all your belongings are there," the officer told her. "All there?"

Merry June nodded, confused and wondering if they were getting her ready to go before the judge. Her shoes were returned to her, and she slipped them on.

"Sign," the policeman pointed to a signature line. He tore off her copy, went back to reading the *Times* and waggled his fingers in her direction. "Have a nice day."

"Can I ask you a question?"

He looked at her over the top of the paper. "One."

"Am I free? What happened?"

"That's two." He shook the Sports section loose from his newspaper and held it in front of his face when he answered, "One, yes, you're free to go. Two, the woman, Tara, took a deal. Ratted out her buddies and told the prosecutor you were just the canary? Know what she meant by that?"

"Yeah. But a canary that lived to tell about it."

TWENTY-NINE

Merry June was more tired than she'd ever been in her entire seventy years. She fell sound asleep in the taxi on her way back to the motel. Once in her room, she bolted the door and ran a hot bath using the miniature bottle of shampoo as bubble bath. She soaked until the water got cold then drained the tub and refilled it a second time. She followed with a long, soapy hot shower. Once she felt like she finally got the jail smell off of her, she put on the soft chenille robe and slippers that Sally had given her. It was three o'clock in the afternoon, so she climbed into bed and flipped on the TV to Dr. Oz.

I'll just rest my eyes for a minute, she thought. She pulled the scratchy brown blanket up to her chin and fell fast asleep.

When she woke up, it was still dark outside. She turned on CNN and climbed out of bed. She was washing up in the bathroom when a news story came on about the game show scandal. With her arms soaped up to her elbows, she hurried back in time to see mug shots of Mac, Ryan, Little Ray and Tara appear on the screen. From what she could tell, coming in at the end of the report, was that the foursome had plans to pull scams on not only *Fortune Hunt* but other game shows as well. The FBI had them in their sights for the past year and were finally able to make their move. When Merry June saw her own mug shot appear on the screen as a person of interest, she fell backwards on the bed and for a minute, watched the room spin around her.

...

Minutes later her cellphone rang. It was Harold. *I can't deal with him right now. So much for keeping this latest disaster a secret.* She decided to ignore the call.

The ringing stopped then started up again. When this continued for a full ten minutes, she took a deep breath and answered. "Hello, Harold."

"Well, Merry June, I see you're still at it."

"Harold, I was a victim I didn't do anything wrong. I was very frightened."

Harold let that slide. "Everyone here thinks you've gone off the deep end. And so do I! Rob is furious and blaming me for letting you go off on this half-cocked adventure. Like I actually LET YOU? Allison isn't speaking to me and Conny and Ed are just plain worried to death."

"I'm sorry everyone's upset, Harold."

"You're sorry? Oh, well then it's all okay because YOU'RE SORRY."

There was a full minute of silence before Merry June whispered, "Harold?"

"What?"

"Can I ask you something?"

"Can I stop you?"

"What does Noah say?" Merry June did feel bad that their nutty mother had embarrassed her children, but it was Noah's reaction that mattered most to her.

"Oh yes, Noah."

"Does he know?"

"He knows. Your damn mug shot is all over television and now it's all over the Internet and YouTube, for God's sake. It looks like some of your fellow *Fortune Hunt* wannabes pulled out their phones to capture," he stopped and coughed when he realized what he said, "to record – the whole ugly incident. You are quite the media darling. I expect you'll get a call from Matt Lauer asking you for an interview."

"I can't believe it. Noah must be mortified. Harold, how can I face him? Will he ever forgive me? This entire trip has been a mess from the get-go."

Another silence followed by a gentle, "Merry June, Noah's not upset."

"What? Did you say he's not upset? How...?"

"He's bragging about you to all his friends. Pulling you up on YouTube to anyone and everyone who will listen. He's telling everybody how cool you are."

Merry June broke out in a sob and had a good cry before Harold could make her listen. "Are you coming home now? Have you had enough because I know damn well I have?"

"Did you mail me the money, my credit card and the plane ticket?"

"There's a problem."

"What? What problem?"

"There wasn't any money in there, Merry June. No plane ticket or credit card either."

"Harold, that's not possible. How can that be? Did you call the hotel?"

"I did and I went down and filled out a claim form for missing property, but the manager didn't hold out much hope."

Merry June held back another sob.

"I'm sorry, honey," said Harold using a term for her she hadn't heard for a very long time.

Things must be really bad, she thought. "Oh, Harold, all I wanted to do was win enough money to buy you that new circular saw you've been wanting and maybe even enough for a trip. It's been a long time since just the two of us went anywhere. And I guess I wanted some excitement, to prove I'm not an old lady no one's ever heard of from a place no one's ever heard of. I wanted to be somebody special, Harold, even if only for thirty minutes. It sounds stupid now when I say it but..."

"It's not stupid, Merry June," he waited, clearing his throat. "I'm sorry I wasn't more supportive. I wish I was there with you now but," he regained his voice, "I'm not. But you are there and here's what we're going to do. First of all, are you in a safe place?"

Merry June looked around at the shabby but secure surroundings. "Yes."

"Okay then, I'm going to wire you enough money to stay a couple more days. Go back to those people at the show and see if you can get another audition. Then I want you to buy another plane ticket and catch the next flight home. I miss you, Merry June and not just because I'm out of dinners and underwear," he chuckled. "But my feet sure do get cold at night."

"Harold, you're my guy," she smiled for the first time in forty-eight hours.

"Go finish what you started—then come home, MJ."

THIRTY

Merry June felt like a woman who'd been given a reprieve from a life sentence. She texted Noah and updated him on everything from her kidnapping, arrest and her last conversation with Harold. Noah replied that all the kids at school were talking about her. "You're the coolest grandma ever," he wrote before signing off.

She walked across the road to McDonald's and jotted down her plans for the rest of her trip. First, she would return to the studio and try to speak with someone about rescheduling her audition. If that failed, well, she would have tried and instead she would just enjoy being a member of the audience. Merry June realized something else too. She wanted to go home. She'd had her adventure but it was time to go back.

An older couple, probably her age, she guessed,

entered with two young children, obviously grandkids, in tow. Grandpa went to the front to order while grandma and the kids got a booth across from Merry June. The kids, a boy and a girl bounced up and down in their seats, excited about spending a day with the grands. Merry June thought about Gigi Madrid and wished she could have a day out like these children.

She watched the family and noticed that both grandparents and grandchildren wore matching white tee shirts with a picture of Mickey Mouse and each of their names embroidered underneath. The little girl, Cindy according to the name on her shirt, kept tugging at her grandma's purse, begging her to let her have whatever it was inside. Grandma finally gave in and took out two sets of black Mouse ears and gave one to each child. Cindy's little brother, Henry, kept snapping the elastic band that held his sister's ears in place. A tussle followed just as Grandpa returned with the food. Things were quiet for a couple of minutes then a childish girl's voice squeaked, "When are we going to see Mickey, Grandpa? Can we go now? Huh?"

Henry joined his sister in the begging. Grandma smiled at Merry June and shrugged, the universal Grandma signal meaning, *what can you do?*

The family left and Merry June watched as the children skipped in front of the adults to the car, on their way to the Happiest Place on Earth.

An elderly woman wearing the McDonald's uniform brought out a mop and a spray bottle of disinfectant and began cleaning up after the family.

"Excuse me," Merry June leaned out of her booth. "How far is Disneyland from here?"

"Not far." Her eyes twinkled at Merry June. "About thirty miles." The woman told her the easiest way for her to get there would be to go to the airport and catch one of the express shuttles that ran continuously to the park. Merry June thanked her and decided that Harold could wait one more day. After all, who knew if she would ever have another chance to see Disneyland?

...

She was getting better at navigating transportation systems. She got to the park with no trouble, paid for a single day pass and arrived at Main Street U.S.A. "It's exactly like in the pictures." She breathed slowly, trying to keep her excitement in rein. The sun was just coming up from behind Cinderella's castle and the view took her breath away.

"I wish I had a camera," she said out loud before she

realized it.

"You can buy a disposable one." An elderly woman standing with a young woman with a baby in a stroller, pointed to one of the many period shops lining the street.

Merry June thanked her and went to do just that. Outside in the brilliant sunlight, she snapped a few photos then hopped on the horse drawn streetcar for the ride to Cinderella's castle. The woman who had directed her to the shops was also on the ride, now without the woman or the baby. She waved at Merry June then proceeded to move over next to her.

"Are you here on your own?" she asked Merry June.

Merry June learned from her recent experiences to be less forthright when talking with perfect strangers, something Allison was always warning her about. "No," she lied, "my family went on ahead to the rides. I'm meeting them in an hour."

"I see," the woman said. She chattered for the remainder of the short ride about the park, the weather, nothing of any consequence and when Merry June got off the bus, she did too.

Merry June had had enough of Californians so she did something that would have been completely uncharacteristic of her only a week ago. She turned and confronted the woman saying, "Please don't follow me anymore. I'm here to enjoy the park and I don't like having you trail around behind me, yakking my head off." It felt good to say her piece but she felt guilty about being rude, so she added, "Have a nice day," and walked off.

Merry June made the mistake of turning around. The woman just stood where she'd left her. She gripped an old fashioned plastic handbag with both hands. She wore a tee shirt that had Tinker Bell emblazoned on the front tucked into shiny, powder blue pants. The ensemble was topped off with the ubiquitous black mouse ears.

What have you done, Merry June Pigg? You've hurt that poor woman's feelings. What kind of person have you become? What would Noah think if he watched his grandma be rude to a stranger who was only trying to be friendly? She debated with herself if she should go back or not. On the one hand, she really did like the freedom of being able to go wherever she wanted, of not having to make polite conversation—although she realized she hadn't exactly done that—and just take in the beauty and excitement of the place—by herself.

She decided to compromise by going back and apologizing. If she didn't do that it would ruin her day as much as having to put up with the woman's company.

Why, just by looking at her, Merry June could tell they had nothing in common.

"Listen," Merry June said approaching the woman, who was still standing where she'd left her, looking forlorn and lonesome. Merry June felt terrible and remembered how alone she'd felt in the hospital, handcuffed to a hospital bed and completely misunderstood. "I'm really sorry I was rude back there. I've had a terrible couple of days and I'm afraid I took it out on you."

The woman brightened.

Merry June offered her hand, "Forgive me?"

She snatched Merry June's hand with both of her own and held it to her breast, scaring the bejeezus out of Merry June.

"Of course, honey. I understand completely. Thank you."

Merry June started to pull away but stepped back. "I'm afraid I also lied to you," she said. She felt herself blush. "I don't have any family here. I'm here by myself." Saying the words made her feel as lonesome as the other woman looked. "I'm truly sorry. I don't know what's gotten into me."

"That's alright, honey." She smiled up at her.

"You see, I only have this one day here and I want to see as much as I can. The day after tomorrow I'm leaving for home and I'll probably never get back here."

"You go on then," the woman told her, "I come here with my daughter and grandson all the time. My older grandson works here so we get a lot of free passes. I love it. Mickey Mouse is the only movie star I would walk across the street to see. I am a huge fan."

Her last comment stopped Merry June in her tracks. Those were the very same words she'd said time and again through the years.

"I wonder," said Merry June slowly, "if I could buy you a drink or something to eat and pick your brain a bit. Since I'm so short on time, I could really use some advice on how to make the most of my day."

"I'd like that," the woman said and introduced herself as Bess.

They picked a shop with outside service where they could enjoy the sights, sounds and smells of Main Street. They both ordered hot chocolate topped with a mountain of whipped cream drizzled over with more chocolate. Bess used Merry June's map of the park to circle the must-see attractions and told her the best times to go to the really busy ones. She laid out a route for her so she

241

wouldn't lose time backtracking and ended the visit with the crown jewel, a chance to get her picture taken with Mickey at his house in Toontown.

"You can see Minnie there too," Bess told her. "Personally though, I don't care for her."

Merry June laughed, wiped whipped cream from her lip and said, "Me either. Mickey deserves better."

They finished their drinks and with Bess's map under her arm, Merry June thanked her and started to leave. Once more, she glanced back at Bess who was gazing into a shop window. *This is silly*, she thought before calling to Bess, "I'd love it if you'd join me. If you want?"

Bess beamed and nodded. "I'll call my daughter and let her know. I can take the Metro home," Bess told Merry June. "I only live fifteen minutes away."

After Bess finished her call, the women headed for Adventure Land where they rode *Pirates of The Caribbean*. Bess asked Merry June if she were game for something a little more exciting and when she answered 'sure' her new friend's face lit up.

"We'll do the *Haunted Mansion* and *Big Thunder Mountain*," she pulled at Merry June who was trotting to keep up. Bess' enthusiasm was rubbing off on Merry June who had been pretty excited to begin with. Since most schools around the country had already resumed classes, the park wasn't crowded and the women sailed through lines with little or no waiting. While they took a short rest break, Merry June told Bess, "I know I wouldn't have had this much fun on my own. Thank you for being my Disneyland guide."

"I'm having a blast," Bess said. "Most of the time I end up riding by myself. My family is tired of the attractions, but not me."

They finished their sodas and Bess pushed back her chair saying, "Next stop, Mickey Mouse." They practically ran to Toontown and neither woman minded waiting in line with kids half their size and a tenth their age. When it was Merry June's turn to be photographed with Mickey, she asked if her friend could be in the picture too.

It was dark by the time they ended the day with a ride on Space Mountain. Merry June had bought a pair of the mouse ears and she imagined how she must look after their roller coaster ride. Bess's ears had slipped to one side and Merry June straightened them, happy that she'd overcome the prejudice she'd felt when she first met Bess. They made their way back to Main Street where Merry June insisted on treating her new friend to dinner.

"I am almost too tired to eat," Merry June said, "but I'm also famished."

When the waiter took their orders, Merry June ordered fried chicken with all the sides. Bess ordered a bowl of chicken rice soup and a coke.

"Oh, Bess, surely you can eat more than that. Aren't you starving?"

Bess shook her head saying, "No, this will be plenty."

Their food came and Merry June dug right in, but Bess just pushed her spoon around the bowl.

"Are you okay?" Merry June asked, worried that she had pushed Bess too hard.

"No, it's okay, really." Bess's face was serious and sad.

Merry June put her fork down on her empty plate, "Tell me what's the matter, Bess."

"We've had such a great time. I've enjoyed being with you so much. I don't want to think of sad things."

"I'd like to think we both made a new friend today," Merry June told her, "and friends share everything, even if they're sad. Especially if they're sad," she added. "Please. I'm a good listener."

Bess set her hat on the chair and took a sip of her drink before she said, "I have chronic kidney failure as a result of diabetes. I've been on dialysis but I need a kidney transplant. I've been on the waiting list for almost a year but there are still a lot of people ahead of me." She wiped her eyes. "I'll never give up hope, but I want to be realistic, to not have a lot of regrets when..." she waited to get her voice back. "Coming here," she looked around at the park, glittering in the warm night air, "helps me forget for a while. After all," she laughed, "this is the 'happiest place on earth.'"

Together the new friends watched the fireworks before the end, as Bess put it, of a 'fantabulous day.'

THIRTY-ONE

The next morning, the bus driver smiled and greeted Merry June as she boarded. He wished her luck when he dropped her off at her usual spot outside the Sony Picture Studios. She threw back her shoulders and walked to the gate. She'd purchased a straw hat with a wide brim at the drug store and pulled it low across her forehead as she approached the entrance. She didn't want to take a chance that the guard might recognize her from television or the newspaper.

The gatekeeper stopped her and asked to see her ticket. She started to explain about her lost suitcase with her plane ticket and all her money and how she'd missed her audition. She left out the part about the fiasco around the audition scam, her arrest and eventual release emphasizing instead the great lengths she'd gone just to get there. The guard held up his hand to stop her when a motorcyclist pulled up alongside of her.

"I'm sorry, Ma'am but if you don't have a ticket, you can't go in. Excuse me," he said turning inside the booth to retrieve a clipboard.

"Good morning, George," he called to the cyclist. The man named George took off his helmet and Merry June had to grab hold of his bike to keep from falling over. She looked into the beautiful brown eyes of none other than the sexiest man alive according to every magazine Merry June could name.

"Are you okay?" There was that famous crooked smile.

"No," she said, "I'm definitely not okay." Her knees shook, her voice shook, everything shook. "Are we having an earthquake?"

Crooked smile. "No. There's no earthquake."

'Gorgeous George' and Merry June could only think of him that way, pulled his bike over to the side of the drive and came back to her, putting his arm around her waist. "Do you need a doctor?" He seemed really worried.

"Are my eyes open? Am I unconscious?"

The brown eyes looked at Ernie, the gatekeeper, and made a signal with his fingers to phone for help.

"Let's just sit you down over here on the grass." He

walked over to the side near his bike. "What's your name?"

"MJ, I mean Merry June."

"Nice to meet you, Merry June." His whole face crinkled deliciously, Merry June thought. "I'm..."

"I know." She started to giggle uncontrollably. "And you're from Maysville. I'm from Shandon," she struggled for words. "Shandon, that's in Ohio. Maysville, though, that's in Kentucky."

"I know." His eyes crinkled some more.

"Of course you do. I feel like an idiot."

"Are you going to see one of the shows, Merry June?"

The words, the built-up tension, and meeting her movie idol came to a head and Merry June just burst into tears. Between weeping, sniffling and gazing into those kind eyes, she told him everything. By the time she was finished, his eyes were wide and his mouth hung open.

"Wow, that's a helluva story, MJ." He waved away the guys in the security vehicle that had responded to Ernie's call.

"I know," she sniffled, "I'm a mess. I'm sorry, I'm keeping you." She offered her hand to shake. "You are every bit as nice as they say you are back home. By the way, my aunt went to school with your aunt. Rosemary, I mean. Western Hills High School. Well, it was wonderful meeting you. Thank you for stopping for me. Goodbye." She smiled and started to walk away.

He looked after her, then called out, "Hey, MJ, why don't you jump on the back of my bike and we'll go see what we can do for a girl from Shandon, Ohio." He helped her fasten the strap on the spare helmet he always carried, steadied her as she lifted her leg over the seat, and drove as slowly as possible to the studio door marked with a large red sign that read *Stage 3.* Merry June still had the disposable camera from Disneyland in her purse so she asked him if he would 'mind very much' posing underneath the sign for a picture.

"I'll do you one better," he said calling to a passerby. "Do you mind?" he asked. "One of my friend MJ and me?"

Merry June felt like she was sleepwalking through the best dream ever. Her famous new friend introduced her to Sandi, one of *Fortune Hunt's* producers, whispered something in her ear that made her blush, then kissed Merry June on the cheek before he walked away. He stopped and turned one more time, giving Merry June a thumb's up.

"Wow, I know it's trite, but can you pinch me?" Merry June asked Sandi, Merry June's guide to behind the scenes.

"Is that 'wow' for the walking away view?" Sandi laughed.

"Definitely part of it." Merry June was ecstatic.

Sandi gave Merry June the backstage tour that included an introduction to the show's star. Merry June asked Willow for her autograph and received a photo of her that she signed 'To Merry June, With love.' At lunch in the studio cafeteria, Merry June was stargazing when she spotted Howie Mandell eating lunch. She texted Noah to tell him she just had a conversation with George and was watching Howie Mandell eating chicken salad.

The afternoon was devoted to taping five shows with short breaks in between. Merry June had to sit in a folding chair at the rear of the studio but the only thing that mattered was she was finally here. She was disappointed that she wasn't able to try out for the show but as she played along with the contestants she was proud at how well she did. *And I didn't need to cheat to do it either. This is a perfect ending to my adventure.* She decided she could be happy for the rest of her life.

When she finally got back to the motel, she was bone tired. It was still early in California, only seven-thirty, but it was ten-thirty at home. She wavered back and forth about calling Harold who went to bed on the stroke of ten every night but she was too excited to keep the day's events to herself.

"I'll call Conny, she'll still be up."

Merry June told her best friend about her day. Conny prodded her for even the smallest details about her meeting with her movie idol and then made her repeat it a second time. "Uh oh," Merry June said, "we've talked through all the bars on my cell phone. I'm going to have to recharge my battery." Both women thought that was just hilarious. They said their goodbyes with Conny exacting a promise from Merry June to call her the second she got home so she could come right over to hear the story all over again.

"See you soon," Merry June rang off.

THIRTY-TWO

Merry June was returning to Culver City from the airport where she'd gone to purchase her plane ticket. A crowd was gathered on the corner opposite the entrance to the studio, so she stopped and asked a man standing there what was going on.

"They're shooting a movie," he told her, "and hiring extras for a crowd scene. Here," he thrust a paper at her. "Fill this out and give it to that guy over there if you're interested."

"What's it about?" she asked.

"I don't know but check out who the Producer is." He nodded at the man across the lot.

Merry June couldn't believe it. She had gazed into those famous eyes only yesterday and here she was with the chance to be in one of his movies. She thought if this wasn't one of Sally's signs, she didn't know what was. She watched as a trio of large, black-suited men hustled him to a waiting limo. Merry June signed her name on the form and gave it to the man in a canary yellow parka with 'Director' printed in black letters across the back. He held a brown folder of the other hopefuls' forms.

"How many people will you be needing?" Merry June asked him.

"A hundred," he said before he looked at her. "Hang around,' he said, sizing her up. "You'll get on." He gave her a yellow card. "Stand right over there." He pointed to where a woman who looked like a movie star was lining people up and handing them cards with black lettering.

Merry June exchanged the yellow card for another card that read, 'bag lady.' She laughed. "Pretty close to the truth."

A young woman in front of her showed Merry June her card assigning her the role of 'woman with backpack.'

The line grew and the extras chatted while they waited. The 'girl with backpack' told Merry June she recently moved to L.A. from Puyallop, Washington and was looking for work. Her graduate degree was in Human Resources, but ever since the economy tanked, she was having no luck finding work in that or any other field. She told Merry June the two hundred dollars pay for extras in this movie would at least pay for a couple of nights in a hostel and a few meals at McDonald's.

"I've even applied there," she told Merry June, referring to McDonald's, "but the manager said he could wallpaper his entire house with applications from people with Master's and even Ph.D. degrees. It's brutal. I might have to go back home to live until I find something. Oh well," she shrugged, "I have a lot of company—unfortunately."

The woman in charge of the extras began going down the line and directing each person, according to their role, to the costume department. From there, they were ushered to make-up and finally to props. Merry June was given an oversized dirty dress, dirty sneakers and a brown wig that was covered with a floral headscarf. It took the makeup man half an hour to add wrinkles and smudge some dirt on her face. She was escorted to props and given a shopping cart stuffed with garbage bags and instructed not to move or touch her face, hair, clothes or the shopping cart. She was led to a bench to wait some more until they received further directions.

"Isn't this exciting?" Merry June said to the young man seated next to her. He looked like a student, and he told Merry June that's what he was in 'real' life.

He said he was enrolled in a graduate program in atmospheric and oceanic studies at UCLA. "I like to pick up one of these gigs when I can. It's fun and I make a little cash. Besides," he tugged Merry June's wig back into place, "I get to meet interesting people, like you."

Merry June told the young man, whose name was Pete, about her family, particularly about Noah.

"What are you doing out here?" Pete asked.

She told him about the things that had happened to her since she left home nearly ten days ago. "I never dreamed that I'd have this grand of an adventure when I started out. It's been an amazing trip. But," she rested her hand on his arm, "The final straw was when I was tricked by a gang of hackers planning to scam..."

"Hey, I saw that story on TV. I thought you looked familiar." When he realized that he just implied Merry June looked like a bag lady even before today, he looked sheepish. She had to laugh at his discomfort.

"I'm sorry," she said, trying not to smear her makeup. "But that was very funny."

"I guess it was," he agreed, red-faced.

"The fact that I'd just spent over sixteen hours in prison," she exaggerated, "probably did make me resemble the lady I am today. In fact, it was probably the reason I landed this role."

The 'girl with backpack' joined Merry June and Pete on the bench. Merry June introduced Pete and the girl told them her name was Emily. The trio passed the time by sharing their stories until it was finally time to shoot the crowd scene.

Everyone was told where to stand and what to do when the Director called for 'Action'. Merry June was instructed to push her shopping cart across an alley while pretending to talk to herself. They repeated the scene several times before the Director called it a day. They returned the props and costumes, received their pay and having put in a full day an exhausted Merry June headed for the bus stop.

...

Merry June was ready to go home. Her bag was packed, her plane booked, and the taxi called. She checked out of the motel, climbed into the cab and looked ahead. "LAX, please," she told the driver.

New TSA scanners were in place when Merry June got in line for the security check. She didn't understand what all the fuss was about and as far as she was concerned, they could scan her, pat her down, go through her bags—whatever it took to keep people safe she thought. She went through the scanner then was asked to step to the side where a female agent explained how she would pat her down, with the back of her hand, then the front. Merry June told her she had an artificial knee, which the agent noted. She was asked to move forward to a table where another agent informed her that he would be searching her backpack and asked her if she had any objection.

"Not at all," Merry June told him. "Go right ahead."

The backpack was searched, Merry June's shoes and belt were returned and she was told to take a seat while the agent spoke with his supervisor. Merry June was puzzled but not concerned as she watched the supervisor and the agent whispering together, conferring over a sheet of paper and looking up at her from time to time. Finally, the supervisor followed by the agent, approached Merry June.

"Good morning," the supervisor greeted her.

"Good morning, Adam," she said, reading his name from the ID pinned to his vest. "Is everything all right?"

"Well," Adam stroked his goatee and stared at Merry June, "we don't know."

Merry June felt panic well up inside. "Why, what's wrong? What did I do? Is it those bottles of shampoos I took from the motel? I thought it was okay. They kept giving me new ones every day. I paid extra for them and the soap too."

That brought a smile to his face. "No, that's not it, Miss Pigg, is it?"

"That's right, only it's Mrs., Mrs. Pigg."

"That's our problem, Mrs. Pigg," the agent said.

"I don't understand," Merry June protested. "What's wrong with my name?" Other passengers who had successfully navigated the currents of security stared at her. She felt like she was guilty of something by the way they looked at her, she just didn't know what.

"I need you to come with me," Adam said, picking up her backpack and taking her by the arm.

"I can't," she pulled away from his grip, "I have to get home. People are expecting me." She checked her watch, "In less than five hours..."

"You'll get your chance to notify your 'people'," he said with emphasis on the word 'people', "but now you need to come with us."

Merry June hadn't noticed the burly security officer who suddenly appeared at Adam's shoulder. Adam took hold of her arm for the second time and pushed her through the crowd. The security officer led them to a service elevator located in the far corner of the concourse.

Seeing the service elevator brought back visions of the one she'd taken the day Ryan and his cohorts had roped her into their scheme. She began having heart palpitations, her palms became sweaty and she could hardly get her breath. "I think I'm having a heart attack," she said.

Her escorts stopped and peered at her closely. "She looks awful pale," the guard, Logan, said.

"She's alright," Adam said, unsure. "I think she's pulling another scam."

Suddenly it dawned on Merry June. They had seen her mug shot on television or the newspaper or any one of a dozen other media outlets. They thought she was a criminal.

"There's a mistake," she cried, clutching Logan's sleeve. "I'm innocent. I was cleared by the police. I was a victim, the canary, they called me."

"Look, Miss,"

"Mrs.," she was screaming now to make them understand, "It's Mrs. Merry June Pigg, you morons."

That didn't sit too well with either Adam or Logan. Getting on either side of her, they picked her up by the elbows, and hustled her into the elevator. Merry June struggled and protested but to no avail. They finally managed to get her through a door marked, 'Security: No Admittance'. Logan locked the door and stood in front of it blocking Merry June's possible attempt at escape. Adam sat behind a large oak desk, gleaming under the green shade of a desk lamp.

"Now, then, Mrs. Pigg. Let's chat."

THIRTY-THREE

"Is this you?" Adam pushed a copy of her mug shot across the surface of the desk.

Merry June nodded without even looking. "You know it is."

He nodded, "Yes, I do. But help me understand something," he said slowly. He smiled at her like he knew something she didn't. "Why does this say you're MJ Wedding?"

"Oh, for cryin' out loud." She was really becoming angry. "I used that as my stage name. Wedding is my maiden name."

Logan snickered and muttered she was pretty long in the tooth for a 'maiden'.

"Show some respect to your elder, then, young man."

Logan looked ashamed but said, "Your stage name? Why do you need a stage name, Mrs. Pigg or MJ Wedding?

Are you an actor?"

Adam shot the man a conspiratorial look.

Merry June stood up and started for the door. "As a matter of fact, *gentlemen,* I just finished a movie produced by a friend of mine."

"Yeah, right, lady. Who's your friend?" Logan growled.

"George Clooney, smarty-pants."

Logan threw back his head and guffawed.

"Play nice, boys and girls," Adam said. "Please, sit back down, Mrs. Pigg. Now, about the name?"

Merry June checked her watch. Her plane left ten minutes ago. She knew there wouldn't be another flight to Cincinnati until ten p.m. *All right, boys,* she thought, *you are about to be treated to the MJ Wedding actors' studio improv. Better buckle up.*

By the time Merry June had finished the story of her adventures—in excruciating detail—an hour and a half had passed. Logan had slid his bulky self down the wall to sit on the floor and Adam's head had long ago dropped to his folded arms on the desk. Once in a while, Merry June would stop her narrative to see if her inquisitors had fallen asleep. She was pretty sure she'd seen Logan's head fall forward onto his chest a couple of times.

"And," she said, "That brings us up to where we are now."

"I don't believe you," Adam said. "Nobody does all that stuff, meets all those weirdos. I'll say this, lady, you got a great imagination. You otta write for television." His laugh was cruel and sarcastic. He wrinkled his nose at her and leaned across the desk. "Aren't you a little, "he paused, "*mature* to be running all over the country. You must think I'm an idiot, Merry June Pigg or MJ Wedding, or whatever it is you're calling yourself today."

"Adam, if that really is your name," she shot back, "the fact that I think you're an idiot is really beside the point."

Adam turned red and Logan stepped forward, his fists balled up.

Adam waved him away and turned back to Merry June. "You got a real smart mouth, lady," he said. He played with the keys on his computer and watched the screens change.

"I'm surprised you even know what smart means, Adam. I know my rights. You can't hold me. I'm an American citizen and I want to go home and," she paused to catch her breath, "I want to go right now or I'm going to start screaming. And," she stood up and got right in his face, feeling his breath hot on her chin, "I'm going to tell this whole airport what you tried to do with me." She watched his face change from fury to shock. "The terrible, terrible things you did. How you, and you," she looked at Logan who couldn't believe what he was hearing, "how the two of you bullied me, manhandled me, roughed up an innocent, old woman who wants nothing more than to go home to her family in Ohio." She hesitated then ripped a button off her blouse for effect. "Now what do you have to say?" She glared at Adam and then at Logan.

"Lady, you're out of your freakin' mind," Logan shouted. "Adam, do something and fast or I'm gettin' the hell outta here and you're on your own. The old bat is crazy."

"Logan, wait a minute. What she said about the *Fortune Hunt* scam is true. I Googled it and she's telling the truth." He stared at his screen.

"Ha. I told you."

Adam ignored her. "The other stuff, well, she's definitely a wacko but apparently she's not a criminal." he rubbed his temples. "I'm going to make an executive decision here."

The guard had his hand on the door, ready to run. "What?"

"We get her out of here. Out of my office, out of my airport, out of my state." He stood and leaned forward, his arms shaking under his weight. "Mrs. Pigg?"

She sat down and smiled sweetly up at him. "Yes?"

"I am going to call down to ticketing and have them re-issue you a ticket for a direct flight to Cincinnati—tonight. Then I'm going to have Logan personally escort you to the gate, bypassing security, and take you directly to the Airport Lounge. He will stay there with you until your flight boards. You'll have access to complimentary beverages, anything you want—snacks, movies, satellite TV, recliners, blankets. We just want you to be comfortable, Mrs. Pigg, capeesh?"

"This has been very trying." She dabbed imaginary tears from her eyes. "I mean a woman of my advanced age. I've already been through so much and this," she looked innocent and forlorn. "I don't know, I mean, what you've offered is—nice."

He glared at her across the desk.

"But..."

"Whadda ya' want, Merry June?"

"Round-trip tickets from Cincinnati to Hawaii for Harold and me."

Adam rubbed his temples and stared daggers at her.

It took him a full minute before he said, "Done. But," he paused, "On one condition."

"What?"

"You never set foot in my airport again."

"Deal."

"Then we're clear." Adam rose from his seat and Logan opened the door.

"Hold it." She decided to press on. "I need one other thing."

Adam's mouth fell open. What more could this woman want. He'd already given away the store.

"I want an apology."

THIRTY-FOUR

Merry June couldn't imagine a more beautiful sight than the lights of her hometown welcoming her back. As the plane banked and crossed the Ohio River above the Greater Cincinnati-Northern Kentucky International Airport, her thoughts were not on her 'great adventure' as she thought of her journey, but rather on the ranch house perched on twenty acres of rolling hills intersected with tributaries from Paddy's Run Creek. She pictured the steam rising off Harold's fishing pond on top of the hill out back and their little black cat, Maizy, who must be wondering why Merry June left her. She imagined Harold waiting for her in Baggage Claim, and then hurrying her along to avoid paying for another hour in the parking garage. *Dorothy was right*, she thought, *there's no place like home*.

The flight attendant collected the newspaper that

Merry June tried to read but couldn't, along with the slippers and the pillow that came with a complimentary glass of wine. "I could get used to this," she quipped to the flight attendant. "I've never flown first class before." The attendant, hurrying to finish her chores prior to landing, ignored Merry June and left her to watch the runway lights brighten as the wheels touched down and the plane screeched to a halt.

The man seated across the aisle from her lifted Merry June's backpack down from the overhead compartment. She wiggled her arms through the straps and waited to deplane.

Travelers with early morning flights were starting to arrive at the gates. Lines formed at Starbucks and McDonalds and the aroma of freshly baked cinnamon buns announced the morning. Merry June walked briskly toward the escalators to the train that would take her to Baggage. She was glad that she was able to skip that last step of waiting for bags to tumble up the ramp onto the carousel. She was the first one off the train and hurried toward the exit. She spotted Harold who searched for her in the crowd of arriving passengers.

"Harold," she yelled to him, any pretense at grandmotherly decorum forgotten. "Harold, here I am—

I'm home," she whispered in his ear, before covering his face with kisses.

Harold, normally shy when it came to public displays of affection, swept his wife into his arms, lifted her off her feet and swung her around in a complete circle before setting her back down. Merry June blushed when she saw people around them smile at their reunion.

Hand in hand they headed to the car and soon were on I-275 heading for home. Harold filled her in on all the things that happened while she was gone; how Conny checked on him every day and waited for Noah to come over after school to show them her latest text, Maizy moping around and waiting for her by the door each evening.

"There's a surprise waiting for you at home," Harold said and smiled.

Try as she might, she couldn't get him to tell so she settled back and watched the scenery that she loved so much; the fields of dry corn and soybeans, the rolling countryside, the mix of pine, cedar, red bud and shag bark hickory trees. It was the most beautiful place in the world, she thought, and she didn't want to leave home for a long time. Even a trip to Hawaii would have to wait until she got her fill of this place—and that might be a while. *I'll let Harold decide about that.*

The sun was bright as they pulled up the drive to the house. Merry June let out a scream when she saw Noah's car parked in the driveway.

She hurried toward the front door as her grandson came out to meet her. "Grandma, I missed you," he planted a big kiss on her cheek and hugged her until she begged him to stop.

"You rascal," she teased, "since when are you up this early?"

"Since the coolest Grandma on the planet was coming home."

Noah always delighted her. She thought that her grandson was the smartest and handsomest and kindest boy in the world. She brushed away the thought that maybe it was just a grandma thing.

She sat at the kitchen table with her 'two favorite men,' she said, but warned Noah not to tell his father. "I'll make some coffee," she said, and started to get up. She stopped when she noticed a look between Harold and Noah.

"You want to wash up?" Harold, asked and, patted her shoulder.

"No, I'm fine."

Harold's raised eyebrows registered his shock. "You relax and catch up with your grandson. I'll take care of the coffee," he added, shocking his wife just as much. "Then you can tell us about your trip."

Noah and Harold sat and listened while she told them every detail of her adventure, about Rufus and Gigi, Sally and Bonny Rose, and the Shepards, "And George," she added with a sigh and an eye roll. "Sooo nice. You can just tell he's a down-to-earth, Mid-western boy under all that Hollywood glitz."

"Grandma," Noah said when she finished, "you should write a book."

THIRTY-FIVE

Merry June arrived home late one October afternoon to find Harold waiting for her at the door. He looked smug and held a large manila envelope in his hands.

"What are you looking so pleased about?"

"I thought you might want to open your mail." He handed her an envelope stamped 'registered mail'. The return address read Sony Picture Studios.

"I wonder why they're writing to me?" She turned the envelope over in her hands. "I hope it has nothing to do with that fiasco at the audition." She held the letter at arm's length like it was a bomb about to explode. "I guess it could be about the movie, but..."

"For God's sake, Merry June," Harold said, "open the damn thing already."

"First I want to call Conny. I told her I wouldn't do anything else without including her." She tried her friend at home and her cell. "No answer. I'll just have to wait. I'll get dinner started. She should be home soon."

Merry June set the envelope on the dining room table and went into the kitchen to start the Cincinnati style chili she'd planned for their dinner. Harold put a pot of water on to boil for the spaghetti and helped himself to one of the brownies he'd baked earlier for their dessert.

"You've become awfully domesticated since I've been gone," she told him and gave him a peck on the cheek.

"I don't want to worry about starving to death the next time you take off," he answered, pinching her on her backside.

"If I do, will you learn how to dust?"

"Sure, if you promise to get me Helen Mirren's autograph."

Harold poured the water off the spaghetti and ladled the chili over it. Merry June topped it off with chopped onions and grated cheese.

"The Shepards told me they tried this once when they were in Cincinnati, but I could tell they weren't impressed."

"Hmm. Which did they try—Gold Star or Skyline?"

Merry June shrugged; her mind was on the contents of the envelope. They finished the meal in silence and

Harold began to clear the dishes.

"Go on," he said gently, "your show's about to come on. I'll clean up."

Merry June went into the family room and sank into the recliner. She looked forward to seeing what new dress Willow would be wearing. When she'd seen her in person, Merry June couldn't believe how tiny she was. "She looked like a little doll," she'd told Harold.

The phone in Merry June's pocket rang. It was Conny saying she'd just gotten home and retrieved her message.

"I tried your cell, Conny."

"Sorry, I forgot to take it with me—again."

Merry June interrupted her and told her about the envelope from the Studios. "If you and Ed come right over, we have plenty of chili and we can open my letter together.

Conny agreed and five minutes later they were walking in the back door with a carton of Graeter's ice cream. Merry June set out the brownies while her friends dug into the chili.

"We can watch *Fortune Hunt* while you guys eat, and then we'll open the letter over dessert," Merry June decided.

Conny and Ed hurried through their meal while

Merry June made a show of loading pots and plates into the dishwasher. "All done?" she asked, when Ed reached for a second helping of chili.

"I guess we are," he answered with a laugh.

"Okay, here goes," she said. She tore into the envelope.

"Read it," Harold told her.

"I can't." She gave it him. "You do it.'

Harold scanned the short letter written on Sony Studios letterhead. A big smile filled out all the creases in his face. "Well, well," he said, "isn't this something?"

"HAROLD," Conny, Ed and Merry June said in unison.

"Read it out loud," Merry June demanded, "I can't take the suspense."

"Okay. 'Dear MJ Wedding.'" He arched his eyebrows at her. "Dear MJ Wedding, You and a guest are invited to attend the premier screening of 'Thumb's Up' in appreciation of your portrayal of 'The Bag Lady'. Please notify the Studios at the phone number below to advise us as to your availability. The Studios will take care of your transportation and hotel accommodations while you are here. Let us know if we can be of further assistance. We look forward to seeing you for this exciting event. Sincerely, Harold Stringer, Chairman &

CEO, Sony Pictures Corporation."

A handwritten postscript read, 'When I spotted my friend from Shandon, Ohio at the screening, I knew it was a 'sign' that we had a hit on our hands. Please come, MJ'. Signed, George C.

Merry June and Conny jumped out of their chairs and hugged, screamed and danced around the room. Ed and Harold watched, amused and pleased, not knowing what to say.

Once the news sank in and everyone settled down, they read and reread the letter.

"You don't think it's a joke, do you?" Merry June asked Harold. "You don't think somebody heard about what happened and did this as a joke? You know what people can do with computers these days. I mean they're always warning us..."

Ed pulled out his cellphone and said, "Let's find out right now. It's only three-thirty on the coast." He paused and asked, "Do you want to go?"

"Are you kidding?" Conny jumped in, "Of course she wants to go."

"Okay, then." He dialed the number on the letter and listened to the electronic answering device. He pushed a number and waited. He grinned and handed her the

276

phone. "Here you go. It's real."

Merry June explained why she was calling and after being forwarded several times, she finally reached the right department. Yes, they told her, they had sent the invitation and would take care of her reservation. The woman on the phone asked who she would be bringing as her guest.

Merry June held the receiver to her chest and looked at Harold. "She wants to know who I'm going to bring. Do you...?"

"No, honey, you know what to do."

Conny nodded in agreement and Ed looked confused.

"My guest will be Noah Pigg," she answered. "I'll take care of his father—later," she said under her breath and gave Harold a happy thumb's up.

...

The night of the premiere Noah wore his father's tuxedo and Merry June wore a new cocktail dress she bought especially for the occasion. This time when it came to shoes, her practical side took over. She wore flats.

Merry June wanted to get to the theatre early so she and Noah could watch the celebrities arrive. She was waiting for one in particular. There was a stir in the crowd when another limo pulled up and the driver opened the door for George Clooney. Noah had his father's fancy camera and began shooting picture after picture.

"George," Noah called as he jumped and waved to get his attention. George was with his beautiful wife and he was giving her all of his attention. Suddenly, Merry June's shawl blew off her shoulders and landed at the woman's feet. George bent down to pick it up and looked around for the owner. It was then he spotted Merry June.

He handed the shawl to her through the crowd. "Hey, MJ, glad you could come. Have fun." He took his wife's arm, turned back at the door, and looking right at Merry June, gave her a thumb's up.

Epilogue

Things were different for the Piggs after Merry June's 'grand adventure'. Harold stopped taking his wife for granted and Merry June stopped trying to teach her 'Pigg' to dance. On their trip to Hawaii, courtesy of LAX, the Piggs relaxed in ways they had not enjoyed for a very long time. Harold even surprised Merry June with a moonlight dinner cruise and wore a flowered, Hawaiian shirt.

...

After they returned home, Merry June and Harold settled down to what they laughingly called their lives as 'hicks in the sticks.' Merry June took a permanent job as a substitute teacher and surprised Harold with that new saw for his workshop. Harold started a small eBay business where he sold handcrafted rocking chairs, baby cribs and even some specialty, one-of-a-kind items to his growing list of customers.

One evening after Harold cleared the dinner table and loaded the dishwasher while Merry June competed with the contestants on *Fortune Hunt*, Noah stopped in for a visit.

"I have something to ask you guys," he said, and pulled a brochure from his jacket pocket. "Summer vacation is almost here," he went on, a twinkle dancing around the corners of his eyes, "And I was thinking it would be cool if..." he paused to open up a pamphlet that read 'Amtrak'. "I mean, I wonder—how would you feel about the three of us taking a train ride? I read where it's a great way to see the country and we studied the Alamo in school and ..."

"What do you say, MJ?" Harold jumped in. He put his arm around his wife's shoulders and smiled. "Are you game?"

"Are you kidding? I say, 'all aboard'."

About the Author

The author is a former geriatric social worker who has been working toward publication while managing a small farm in Butler County with her husband. Witte's experiences with older adults and life in a rural community have provided the inspiration for *M$. Fortune*.

Other books by Kandy Witte, DBA, Lou Fletcher; *Bingo-You're Dead (Volume 1, Murder Is My Game); Mahjong Is Murder (Volume 2, Murder Is My Game)* coming Spring, 2015.